Five Stories by Willa Cather

WILLA CATHER

Five Stories

WITH AN ARTICLE BY GEORGE N. KATES

ON MISS CATHER'S LAST,

UNFINISHED, AND UNPUBLISHED

AVIGNON STORY

VINTAGE BOOKS

A DIVISION OF RANDOM HOUSE

New York

CONTENTS

Five Stories by Willa Cather

The Enchanted Bluff*

WE HAD our swim before sundown, and while we were cooking our supper the oblique rays of light made a dazzling glare on the white sand about us. The translucent red ball itself sank behind the brown stretches of corn field as we sat down to eat, and the warm layer of air that had rested over the water and our clean sand-bar grew fresher and smelled of the rank ironweed and sunflowers growing on the flatter shore. The river was brown and sluggish, like any other of the half-dozen streams that water the Nebraska corn lands. On one shore was an irregular line of bald clay bluffs where a few scrub-oaks with thick trunks and flat, twisted tops threw light shadows on the long grass. The western shore was low and level, with corn fields that stretched to the sky-line, and all along the water's edge were little sandy coves and beaches where slim cottonwoods and willow saplings flickered.

The turbulence of the river in springtime discour-

* Published in *Harper's Magazine*, April 1909.

aged milling, and, beyond keeping the old red bridge in repair, the busy farmers did not concern themselves with the stream; so the Sandtown boys were left in undisputed possession. In the autumn we hunted quail through the miles of stubble and fodder land along the flat shore, and, after the winter skating season was over and the ice had gone out, the spring freshets and flooded bottoms gave us our great excitement of the year. The channel was never the same for two successive seasons. Every spring the swollen stream undermined a bluff to the east, or bit out a few acres of corn field to the west and whirled the soil away to deposit it in spumy mud banks somewhere else. When the water fell low in midsummer, new sand-bars were thus exposed to dry and whiten in the August sun. Sometimes these were banked so firmly that the fury of the next freshet failed to unseat them; the little willow seedlings emerged triumphantly from the yellow froth, broke into spring leaf, shot up into summer growth, and with their mesh of roots bound together the moist sand beneath them against the batterings of another April. Here and there a cottonwood soon glittered among them, quivering in the low current of air that, even on breathless days when the dust hung like smoke above the wagon road, trembled along the face of the water.

It was on such an island, in the third summer of its yellow green, that we built our watch-fire; not in the thicket of dancing willow wands, but on the level terrace of fine sand which had been added that spring; a little new bit of world, beautifully ridged with ripple marks, and strewn with the tiny skeletons of turtles and fish, all as white and dry as if they had been expertly cured. We had been careful not to mar the freshness of the place, although we often swam to it on summer evenings and lay on the sand to rest.

This was our last watch-fire of the year, and there

were reasons why I should remember it better than any of the others. Next week the other boys were to file back to their old places in the Sandtown High School, but I was to go up to the Divide to teach my first country school in the Norwegian district. I was already homesick at the thought of quitting the boys with whom I had always played; of leaving the river, and going up into a windy plain that was all windmills and corn fields and big pastures; where there was nothing wilful or unmanageable in the landscape, no new islands, and no chance of unfamiliar birds—such as often followed the watercourses.

Other boys came and went and used the river for fishing or skating, but we six were sworn to the spirit of the stream, and we were friends mainly because of the river. There were the two Hassler boys, Fritz and Otto, sons of the little German tailor. They were the youngest of us; ragged boys of ten and twelve, with sunburned hair, weather-stained faces, and pale blue eyes. Otto, the elder, was the best mathematician in school, and clever at his books, but he always dropped out in the spring term as if the river could not get on without him. He and Fritz caught the fat, horned catfish and sold them about the town, and they lived so much in the water that they were as brown and sandy as the river itself.

There was Percy Pound, a fat, freckled boy with chubby cheeks, who took half a dozen boys' story-papers and was always being kept in for reading detective stories behind his desk. There was Tip Smith, destined by his freckles and red hair to be the buffoon in all our games, though he walked like a timid little old man and had a funny, cracked laugh. Tip worked hard in his father's grocery store every afternoon, and swept it out before school in the morning. Even his recreations were laborious. He collected cigarette cards and tin tobacco-tags indefatigably, and would sit for hours humped up over a snarling little scroll-saw which he kept in his attic. His dearest possessions were some little pill-bottles that purported to contain grains of wheat from the Holy Land, water from the Jordan and the Dead Sea, and earth from the Mount of Olives. His father had bought these dull things from a Baptist missionary who peddled them, and Tip seemed to derive great satisfaction from their remote origin.

The tall boy was Arthur Adams. He had fine hazel eyes that were almost too reflective and sympathetic for a boy, and such a pleasant voice that we all loved to hear him read aloud. Even when he had to read poetry aloud at school, no one ever thought of laughing. To be sure, he was not at school very much of the time. He was seventeen and should have finished the High School the year before, but he was always off somewhere with his gun. Arthur's mother was dead, and his father, who was feverishly absorbed in promoting schemes, wanted to send the boy away to school and get him off his hands; but Arthur always begged off for another year and promised to study. I remember him as a tall, brown boy with an intelligent face, always lounging among a lot of us little fellows, laughing at us oftener than with us, but such a soft, satisfied laugh that we felt rather flattered when we provoked it. In after-years people said that Arthur had been given to evil ways even as a lad, and it is true that we often saw him with the gambler's sons and with old Spanish Fanny's boy, but if he learned anything ugly in their company he never betrayed it to us. We would have followed Arthur anywhere, and I am bound to say that he led us into no worse places than the cat-tail marshes and the stubble fields. These, then, were the boys who camped with me that summer night upon the sand-bar.

After we finished our supper we beat the willow

thicket for driftwood. By the time we had collected enough, night had fallen, and the pungent, weedy smell from the shore increased with the coolness. We threw ourselves down about the fire and made another futile effort to show Percy Pound the Little Dipper. We had tried it often before, but he could never be got past the big one.

"You see those three big stars just below the handle, with the bright one in the middle?" said Otto Hassler; "that's Orion's belt, and the bright one is the clasp." I crawled behind Otto's shoulder and sighted up his arm to the star that seemed perched upon the tip of his steady forefinger. The Hassler boys did seine-fishing at night, and they knew a good many stars.

Percy gave up the Little Dipper and lay back on the sand, his hands clasped under his head. "I can see the North Star," he announced, contentedly, pointing toward it with his big toe. "Anyone might get lost and need to know that."

We all looked up at it.

"How do you suppose Columbus felt when his compass didn't point north any more?" Tip asked.

Otto shook his head. "My father says that there was another North Star once, and that maybe this one won't last always. I wonder what would happen to us down here if anything went wrong with it?"

Arthur chuckled. "I wouldn't worry, Ott. Nothing's apt to happen to it in your time. Look at the Milky Way! There must be lots of good dead Indians."

We lay back and looked, meditating, at the dark cover of the world. The gurgle of the water had become heavier. We had often noticed a mutinous, complaining note in it at night, quite different from its cheerful daytime chuckle, and seeming like the voice of a much deeper and more powerful stream.

Our water had always these two moods: the one of sunny complaisance, the other of inconsolable, passionate regret.

"Queer how the stars are all in sort of diagrams," remarked Otto. "You could do most any proposition in geometry with 'em. They always look as if they meant something. Some folks say everybody's fortune is all written out in the stars, don't they?"

"They believe so in the old country," Fritz affirmed.

But Arthur only laughed at him. "You're thinking of Napoleon, Fritzey. He had a star that went out when he began to lose battles. I guess the stars don't keep any close tally on Sandtown folks."

We were speculating on how many times we could count a hundred before the evening star went down behind the corn fields, when someone cried, "There comes the moon, and it's as big as a cart wheel!"

We all jumped up to greet it as it swam over the bluffs behind us. It came up like a galleon in full sail; an enormous, barbaric thing, red as an angry heathen god.

"When the moon came up red like that, the Aztecs used to sacrifice their prisoners on the temple top," Percy announced.

"Go on, Perce. You got that out of *Golden Days*. Do you believe that, Arthur?" I appealed.

Arthur answered, quite seriously: "Like as not. The moon was one of their gods. When my father was in Mexico City he saw the stone where they used to sacrifice their prisoners."

As we dropped down by the fire again some one asked whether the Mound-Builders were older than the Aztecs. When we once got upon the Mound-Builders we never willingly got away from them, and we were still conjecturing when we heard a loud splash in the water.

"Must have been a big cat jumping," said Fritz. "They do sometimes. They must see bugs in the dark. Look what a track the moon makes!"

There was a long, silvery streak on the water, and where the current fretted over a big log it boiled up like gold pieces.

"Suppose there ever *was* any gold hid away in this old river?" Fritz asked. He lay like a little brown Indian, close to the fire, his chin on his hand and his bare feet in the air. His brother laughed at him, but Arthur took his suggestion seriously.

"Some of the Spaniards thought there was gold up here somewhere. Seven cities chuck full of gold, they had it, and Coronado and his men came up to hunt it. The Spaniards were all over this country once."

Percy looked interested. "Was that before the Mormons went through?"

We all laughed at this.

"Long enough before. Before the Pilgrim Fathers, Perce. Maybe they came along this very river. They always followed the watercourses."

"I wonder where this river really does begin?" Tip mused. That was an old and a favorite mystery which the map did not clearly explain. On the map the little black line stopped somewhere in western Kansas; but since rivers generally rose in mountains, it was only reasonable to suppose that ours came from the Rockies. Its destination, we knew, was the Missouri, and the Hassler boys always maintained that we could embark at Sandtown in floodtime, follow our noses, and eventually arrive at New Orleans. Now they took up their old argument. "If us boys had grit enough to try it, it wouldn't take no time to get to Kansas City and St. Joe."

We began to talk about the places we wanted to go to. The Hassler boys wanted to see the stock-yards in Kansas City, and Percy wanted to see a big store in Chicago. Arthur was interlocutor and did not betray himself.

"Now it's your turn, Tip."

Tip rolled over on his elbow and poked the fire, and his eyes looked shyly out of his queer, tight little face. "My place is awful far away. My Uncle Bill told me about it."

Tip's Uncle Bill was a wanderer, bitten with mining fever, who had drifted into Sandtown with a broken arm, and when it was well had drifted out again.

"Where is it?"

"Aw, it's down in New Mexico somewheres. There aren't no railroads or anything. You have to go on mules, and you run out of water before you get there and have to drink canned tomatoes."

"Well, go on, kid. What's it like when you do get there?"

Tip sat up and excitedly began his story.

"There's a big red rock there that goes right up out of the sand for about nine hundred feet. The country's flat all around it, and this here rock goes up all by itself, like a monument. They call it the Enchanted Bluff down there, because no white man has ever been on top of it. The sides are smooth rock, and straight up, like a wall. The Indians say that hundreds of years ago, before the Spaniards came, there was a village away up there in the air. The tribe that lived there had some sort of steps, made out of wood and bark, hung down over the face of the bluff, and the braves went down to hunt and carried water up in big jars swung on their backs. They kept a big supply of water and dried meat up there, and never went down except to hunt. They were a peaceful tribe that made cloth and pottery, and they went up there to get out of the wars. You see, they could pick off any war party that tried to get up their little steps. The Indians say they were a handsome people, and they had some sort of queer religion. Uncle Bill thinks they were Cliff-Dwellers who had got into trouble and left home. They weren't fighters, anyhow.

"One time the braves were down hunting and an awful storm came up—a kind of waterspout—and when they got back to their rock they found their little staircase had been all broken to pieces, and only a few steps were left hanging away up in the air. While they were camped at the foot of the rock, wondering what to do, a war party from the north came along and massacred 'em to a man, with all the old folks and women looking on from the rock. Then the war party went on south and left the village to get down the best way they could. Of course they never got down. They starved to death up there, and when the war party came back on their way north, they could hear the children crying from the edge of the bluff where they had crawled out, but they didn't see a sign of a grown Indian, and nobody has ever been up there since."

We exclaimed at this dolorous legend and sat up.

"There couldn't have been many people up there," Percy demurred. "How big is the top, Tip?"

"Oh, pretty big. Big enough so that the rock doesn't look nearly as tall as it is. The top's bigger than the base. The bluff is sort of worn away for several hundred feet up. That's one reason it's so hard to climb."

I asked how the Indians got up, in the first place.

"Nobody knows how they got up or when. A hunting party came along once and saw that there was a town up there, and that was all."

Otto rubbed his chin and looked thoughtful. "Of

course there must be some way to get up there. Couldn't people get a rope over someway and pull a ladder up?"

Tip's little eyes were shining with excitement. "I know a way. Me and Uncle Bill talked it all over. There's a kind of rocket that would take a rope over —life-savers use 'em—and then you could hoist a rope-ladder and peg it down at the bottom and make it tight with guy-ropes on the other side. I'm going to climb that there bluff, and I've got it all planned out."

Fritz asked what he expected to find when he got up there.

"Bones, maybe, or the ruins of their town, or pottery, or some of their idols. There might be 'most anything up there. Anyhow, I want to see."

"Sure nobody else has been up there, Tip?" Arthur asked.

"Dead sure. Hardly anybody ever goes down there. Some hunters tried to cut steps in the rock once, but they didn't get higher than a man can reach. The Bluff's all red granite, and Uncle Bill thinks it's a boulder the glaciers left. It's a queer place, anyhow. Nothing but cactus and desert for hundreds of miles, and yet right under the Bluff there's good water and plenty of grass. That's why the bison used to go down there."

Suddenly we heard a scream above our fire, and jumped up to see a dark, slim bird floating southward far above us—a whooping-crane, we knew by her cry and her long neck. We ran to the edge of the island, hoping we might see her alight, but she wavered southward along the rivercourse until we lost her. The Hassler boys declared that by the look of the heavens it must be after midnight, so we threw more wood on our fire, put on our jackets, and curled down in the warm sand. Several of us pretended to doze, but I fancy we were really thinking about Tip's Bluff and the extinct people. Over in the wood the ring-doves were calling mournfully to one another, and once we heard a dog bark, far away. "Somebody getting into old Tommy's melon patch," Fritz murmured sleepily, but nobody answered him. By and by Percy spoke out of the shadows.

"Say, Tip, when you go down there will you take me with you?"

"Maybe."

"Suppose one of us beats you down there, Tip?"

"Whoever gets to the Bluff first has got to promise to tell the rest of us exactly what he finds," remarked one of the Hassler boys, and to this we all readily assented.

Somewhat reassured, I dropped off to sleep. I must have dreamed about a race for the Bluff, for I awoke in a kind of fear that other people were getting ahead of me and that I was losing my chance. I sat up in my damp clothes and looked at the other boys, who lay tumbled in uneasy attitudes about the dead fire. It was still dark, but the sky was blue with the last wonderful azure of night. The stars glistened like crystal globes, and trembled as if they shone through a depth of clear water. Even as I watched, they began to pale and the sky brightened. Day came suddenly, almost instantaneously. I turned for another look at the blue night, and it was gone. Everywhere the birds began to call, and all manner of little insects began to chirp and hop about in the willows. A breeze sprang up from the west and brought the heavy smell of ripened corn. The boys rolled over and shook themselves. We stripped and plunged into the river just as the sun came up over the windy bluffs.

When I came home to Sandtown at Christmas time, we skated out to our island and talked over the whole project of the Enchanted Bluff, renewing our resolution to find it.

Although that was twenty years ago, none of us have ever climbed the Enchanted Bluff. Percy Pound is a stockbroker in Kansas City and will go nowhere that his red touring-car cannot carry him. Otto Hassler went on the railroad and lost his foot braking; after which he and Fritz succeeded their father as the town tailors.

Arthur sat about the sleepy little town all his life— he died before he was twenty-five. The last time I saw him, when I was home on one of my college vacations, he was sitting in a steamer-chair under a cottonwood tree in the little yard behind one of the two Sandtown saloons. He was very untidy and his hand was not steady, but when he rose, unabashed, to greet me, his eyes were as clear and warm as ever. When I had talked with him for an hour and heard him laugh again, I wondered how it was that when Nature had taken such pains with a man, from his hands to the arch of his long foot, she had ever lost him in Sandtown. He joked about Tip Smith's Bluff, and declared he was going down there just as soon as the weather got cooler; he thought the Grand Canyon might be worth while, too.

I was perfectly sure when I left him that he would never get beyond the high plank fence and the comfortable shade of the cottonwood. And, indeed, it was under that very tree that he died one summer morning.

Tip Smith still talks about going to New Mexico. He married a slatternly, unthrifty country girl, has been much tied to a perambulator, and has grown stooped and gray from irregular meals and broken sleep. But the worst of his difficulties are now over, and he has, as he says, come into easy water. When

I was last in Sandtown I walked home with him late one moonlight night, after he had balanced his cash and shut up his store. We took the long way around and sat down on the schoolhouse steps, and between us we quite revived the romance of the lone red rock and the extinct people. Tip insists that he still means to go down there, but he thinks now he will wait until his boy Bert is old enough to go with him. Bert has been let into the story, and thinks of nothing but the Enchanted Bluff.

Tom Outland's Story*

ONE/   The thing that side-tracked me and made me so late coming to college was a somewhat unusual accident, or string of accidents. It began with a poker game, when I was a call boy in Pardee, New Mexico.

One cold, clear night in the fall I started out to hunt up a freight crew that was to go out soon after midnight. It was just after pay day, and one of the fellows had tipped me off that there would be a poker game going on in the card-room behind the Ruby Light saloon. I knew most of my crew would be there, except Conductor Willis, who had a sick baby at home. The front windows were dark, of course. I went up the back alley, through a tumble-down ice house and a court, into a 'dobe room that didn't open into the saloon proper at all. It was crowded, and hot and stuffy enough. There were six or seven in the game, and a crowd of fellows were standing about the walls, rubbing the white-wash off on to their coat shoulders. There was a

* From *The Professor's House*, 1925.

16

bird-cage hanging in one window, covered with an old flannel shirt, but the canary had wakened up and was singing away for dear life. He was a beautiful singer—an old Mexican had trained him —and he was one of the attractions of the place.

I happened along when a jack-pot was running. Two of the fellows I'd come for were in it, and they naturally wanted to finish the hand. I stood by the door with my watch, keeping time for them. Among the players I saw two sheep men who always liked a lively game, and one of the bystanders told me you had to buy a hundred dollars' worth of chips to get in that night. The crowd was fussing about one fellow, Rodney Blake, who had come in from his engine without cleaning up. That wasn't customary; the minute a man got in from his run, he took a bath, put on citizen's clothes, and went to a barber. This Blake was a new fireman on our division. He'd come up town in his greasy overalls and sweaty blue shirt, with his face streaked up with smoke. He'd been drinking; he smelled of it, and his eyes were out of focus. All the other men were clean and freshly shaved, and they were sore at Blake—said his hands were so greasy they marked the cards. Some of them wanted to put him out of the game, but he was a big, heavy-built fellow, and nobody wanted to be the man to do it. It didn't please them any better when he took the jack-pot.

I got my two men and hurried them out, and two others from the row along the wall took their places. One of the chaps who left with me asked me to go up to his house and get his grip with his work clothes. He'd lost every cent of his pay cheque and didn't want to face his wife. I asked him who was winning.

"Blake. The dirty boomer's been taking everything. But the fellows will clean him out before morning."

About two o'clock, when my work for that night was over and I was going home to sleep, I just dropped in at the card-room to see how things had come out. The game was breaking up. Since I left them at midnight, they had changed to stud poker, and Blake, the fireman, had cleaned everybody out. He was cashing in his chips when I came in. The bank was a little short, but Blake made no fuss about it. He had something over sixteen hundred dollars lying on the table before him in banknotes and gold. Some of the crowd were insulting him, trying to get him into a fight and loot him. He paid no attention and began to put the money away, not looking at anybody. The bills he folded and put inside the band of his hat. He filled his overalls pockets with the gold, and swept the rest of it into his big red neckerchief.

I'd been interested in this fellow ever since he came on our division; he was close-mouthed and un-friendly. He was one of those fellows with a settled, mature body and a young face, such as you often see among working-men. There was something calm, and sarcastic, and mocking about his expression—that, too, you often see among working-men. When he had put all his money away, he got up and walked toward the door without a word, without saying good-night to anybody.

"Manners of a hog, and a dirty hog!" little Barney Shea yelled after him. Blake's back was just in the doorway; he hitched up one shoulder, but didn't turn or make a sound.

I slipped out after him and followed him down the street. His walk was unsteady, and the gold in his baggy overalls pockets clinked with every step he took. I ran a little way and caught up with him. "What are you going to do with all that money, Blake?" I asked him.

"Lose it, to-morrow night. I'm no hog for money. Damned barber-pole dudes!"

I thought I'd better follow him home. I knew he lodged with an old Mexican woman, in the yellow quarter, behind the round-house. His room opened on to the street, by a sky-blue door. He went in, didn't strike a light or make a stab at undressing, but threw himself just as he was on the bed and went to sleep. His hat stuck between the iron rods of the bed-head, the gold ran out of his pockets and rolled over the bare floor in the dark.

I struck a match and lit a candle. The bed took up half the room; on the dresser was a grip with his clean clothes in it, just as he'd brought it in from his run. I took out the clothes and began picking up the money; got the bills out of his hat, emptied his pockets, and collected the coins that lay in the hollow of the bed about his hips, and put it all into the grip. Then I blew out the light and sat down to listen. I trusted all the boys who were at the Ruby Light that night, except Barney Shea. He might try to pull something off on a stranger, down in Mexican town. We had a quiet night, however, and a cold one. I found Blake's winter overcoat hanging on the wall and wrapped up in it. I wasn't a bit sorry when the roosters began to crow and the dogs began barking all over Mexican town. At last the sun came up and turned the desert and the 'dobe town red in a minute. I began to shake the man on the bed. Waking men who didn't want to get up was part of my job, and I didn't let up on him until I had him on his feet.

"Hello, kid, come to call me?"

I told him I'd come to call him to a Harvey House breakfast. "You owe me a good one. I brought you home last night."

"Sure, I'm glad to have company. Wait till I

19

wash up a bit." He took his soap and towel and comb and went out into the patio, a neat little sanded square with flowers and vines all around, and washed at the trough under the pump. Then he called me to come and pump water on his head. After he'd stood the gush of cold water for a few seconds, he straightened up with his teeth chattering.

"That ought to get the whisky out of a fellow's head, oughtn't it? Felt good, Tom." Presently he began feeling his side pockets. "Was I dreaming something, or did I take a string of jack-pots last night?"

"The money's in your grip," I told him. "You don't deserve it, for you were too drunk to take care of it. I had to come after you and pick it up out of the mud."

"All right. I'll go halvers. Easy come, easy go."

I told him I didn't want anything off him but breakfast, and I wanted that pretty soon.

"Go easy, son. I've got to change my shirt. This one's wet."

"It's worse than wet. You oughtn't to go up town without changing. You're a stranger here, and it makes a bad impression."

He shrugged his shoulders and looked superior. He had a square-built, honest face and steady eyes that didn't carry a cynical expression very well. I knew he was a decent chap, though he'd been drinking and acting ugly ever since he'd been on our division.

After breakfast we went out and sat in the sun at a place where the wooden sidewalk ran over a sand gully and made a sort of bridge. I had a long talk with him. I was carrying the grip with his winnings in it, and I finally persuaded him to go with me to the bank. We put every cent of it into a savings account that he couldn't touch for a year.

From that night Blake and I were fast friends. He was the sort of fellow who can do anything for somebody else, and nothing for himself. There are lots like that among working-men. They aren't trained by success to a sort of systematic selfishness. Rodney had been unlucky in personal relations. He'd run away from home when he was a kid because his mother married again—a man who had been paying attention to her while his father was still alive. He got engaged to a girl down on the Southern Pacific, and she double-crossed him, as he said. He went to Old Mexico and let his friends put all his savings into an oil well, and they skinned him. What he needed was a pal, a straight fellow to give an account to. I was ten years younger, and that was an advantage. He liked to be an older brother. I suppose the fact that I was a kind of stray and had no family made it easier for him to unbend to me. He surely got to think a lot of me, and I did of him. It was that winter I had pneumonia. Mrs. O'Brien couldn't do much for me; she was overworked, poor woman, with a houseful of children. Blake took me down to his room, and he and the old Mexican woman nursed me. He ought to have had boys of his own to look after. Nature's full of such substitutions, but they always seem to me sad, even in botany.

I wasn't able to be about until spring, and then the doctor and Father Duchene said I must give up night work and live in the open all summer. Before I knew anything about it, Blake had thrown up his job on the Santa Fé, and got a berth for him and me with the Sitwell Cattle Company. Jonas Sitwell was one of the biggest cattle men in our part of New Mexico. Roddy and I were to ride the range with a bunch of grass cattle all summer, then take them down to a winter camp on the Cruzados river and keep them on pasture until spring.

We went out about the first of May, and joined our cattle twenty miles south of Pardee, down toward the Blue Mesa. The Blue Mesa was one of the landmarks we always saw from Pardee—landmarks mean so much in a flat country. To the northwest, over toward Utah, we had the Mormon Buttes, three sharp blue peaks that always sat there. The Blue Mesa was south of us, and was much stronger in colour, almost purple. People said the rock itself had a deep purplish cast. It looked, from our town, like a naked blue rock set down alone in the plain, almost square, except that the top was higher at one end. The old settlers said nobody had ever climbed it, because the sides were so steep and the Cruzados river wound round it at one end and under-cut it.

Blake and I knew that the Sitwell winter camp was down on the Cruzados river, directly under the mesa, and all summer long, while we drifted about with our cattle from one water-hole to another, we planned how we were going to climb the mesa and be the first men up there. After supper, when we lit our pipes and watched the sunset, climbing the mesa was our staple topic of conversation. Our job was a cinch; the actual work wouldn't have kept one man busy. The Sitwell people were good to their hands. John Rapp, the foreman, came along once a month in his spring-wagon, to see how the cattle were doing and to bring us supplies and bundles of old newspapers.

Blake was a conscientious reader of newspapers. He always wanted to know what was going on in the world, though most of it displeased him. He brooded on the great injustices of his time; the hanging of the Anarchists in Chicago, which he could just remember, and the Dreyfus case. We had long arguments about what we read in the papers, but we never quarrelled. The only trouble I had with Blake was in getting to do my share of the work. He made my health a pretext for taking all the heavy chores, long after I was as well as he was. I'd brought my Cæsar along, and had promised Father Duchene to read a hundred lines a day. Blake saw that I did it—made me translate the dull stuff aloud to him. He said if I once knew Latin, I wouldn't have to work with my back all my life like a burro. He had great respect for education, but he believed it was some kind of hocus-pocus that enabled a man to live without work. We had *Robinson Crusoe* with us, and Roddy's favourite book, *Gulliver's Travels*, which he never tired of.

Late in October, Rapp, the foreman, came along to accompany us down to the winter camp. Blake stayed with the cattle about fifteen miles to the east, where the grass was still good, and Rapp and I went down to air out the cabin and stow away our winter supplies.

TWO/ The cabin stood in a little grove of piñons, about thirty yards back from the Cruzados river, facing south and sheltered on the north by a low hill. The grama grass grew right up to the doorstep, and the rabbits were running about and the grasshoppers hitting the door when we pulled up and looked at the place. There was no litter around, it was as clean as a prairie-dog's house. No outbuildings, except a shed for our horses. The hill-side behind was sandy and covered with tall clumps of deer-horn cactus, but there was nothing but grass to the south, with streaks of bright yellow rabbitbrush. Along the river the cottonwoods and quaking asps had already turned gold. Just across from us, overhanging us, indeed, stood the mesa, a pile of purple rock, all broken out with red sumach and yellow aspens up in the high crevices of the cliffs. From the cabin, night and day, you could hear the river, where it made a bend round the foot of the mesa and churned over the rocks. It was the sort of place a man would like to stay in forever.

I helped Rapp open the wooden shutters and sweep out the cabin. We put clean blankets on the bunks, and stowed away bacon and coffee and canned stuff on the shelves behind the cook-stove. I confess I looked forward to cooking on an iron stove with four holes. Rapp explained to me that Blake and I wouldn't be able to enjoy all this luxury together for a time. He wanted the herd kept some distance to the north as long as the grass held out up there, and Roddy and I could take turn about, one camping near the cattle and one sleeping in a bed.

"There's not pasture enough down here to take them through a long winter," he said, "and it's safest to keep them grazing up north while you can. Besides, if you bring them down here while the weather's so warm, they get skittish, and that mesa over there makes trouble. They swim the river and bolt into the mesa, and that's the last you ever see of them. We've lost a lot of critters that way. The mesa has been populated by run-aways from our herd, till now there's a fine bunch of wild cattle up there. When the wind's right, our cows over here get the scent of them and make a break for the river. You'll have to watch 'em close when you bring 'em down."

I asked him whether nobody had ever gone over to get the lost cattle out.

Rapp glared at me. "Out of that mesa? Nobody has ever got into it yet. The cliffs are like the base of a monument, all the way round. The only way into it is through that deep canyon that opens on the water level, just where the river makes the bend.

You can't get in by that, because the river's too deep to ford and too swift to swim. Oh, I suppose a horse could swim it, if cattle can, but I don't want to be the man to try."

I remarked that I had had my eye on the mesa all summer and meant to climb it.

"Not while you're working for the Sitwell Company, you don't! If you boys try any nonsense of that sort, I'll fire you quick. You'd break your bones and lose the herd for us. You have to watch them close to keep them from going over, I tell you. If it wasn't for that mesa, this would be the best winter range in all New Mexico."

After the foreman left us, we settled down to easy living and fine weather; blue and gold days, and clear, frosty nights. We kept the cattle off to the north and east and alternated in taking charge of them. One man was with the herd while the other got his sleep and did the cooking at the cabin. The mesa was our only neighbour, and the closer we got to it, the more tantalizing it was. It was no longer a blue, featureless lump, as it had been from a distance. Its sky-line was like the profile of a big beast lying down; the head to the north, higher than the flanks around which the river curved. The north end we could easily believe impassable—sheer cliffs that fell from the summit to the plain, more than a thousand feet. But the south flank, just across the river from us, looked accessible by way of the deep canyon that split the bulk in two, from the top rim to the river, then wound back into the solid cube so that it was invisible at a distance, like a mouse track winding into a big cheese. This canyon didn't break the solid outline of the mesa, and you had to be close to see that it was there at all. We faced the mesa on its shortest side; it was only about three miles long from north to south, but east and west it measured nearly twice that distance. Whether the top was wooded we couldn't see—it was too high above us; but the cliffs and canyon on the river side were fringed with beautiful growth, groves of quaking asps and piñons and a few dark cedars, perched up in the air like the hanging gardens of Babylon. At certain hours of the day, those cedars, growing so far up on the rocks, took on the bluish tint of the cliffs themselves.

It was light up there long before it was with us. When I got up at daybreak and went down to the river to get water, our camp would be cold and grey, but the mesa top would be red with sunrise, and all the slim cedars along the rocks would be gold —metallic, like tarnished gold-foil. Some mornings it would loom up above the dark river like a blazing volcanic mountain. It shortened our days, too, considerably. The sun got behind it early in the afternoon, and then our camp would lie in its shadow. After a while the sunset colour would begin to stream up from behind it. Then the mesa was like one great ink-black rock against a sky on fire.

No wonder the thing bothered us and tempted us; it was always before us, and was always changing. Black thunder-storms used to roll up from behind it and pounce on us like a panther without warning. The lightning would play round it and jab into it so that we were always expecting it would fire the brush. I've never heard thunder so loud as it was there. The cliffs threw it back at us, and we thought the mesa itself, though it seemed so solid, must be full of deep canyons and caverns, to account for the prolonged growl and rumble that followed every crash of thunder. After the burst in the sky was over, the mesa went on sounding like a drum, and seemed itself to be muttering and making noises.

One afternoon I was out hunting turkeys. Just

as the sun was getting low, I came through a sea of rabbit-brush, still yellow, and the horizontal rays of light, playing into it, brought out the contour of the ground with great distinctness. I noticed a number of straight mounds, like plough furrows, running from the river inland. It was too late to examine them. I cut a scrub willow and stuck a stake into one of the ridges, to mark it. The next day I took a spade down to the plantation of rabbit-brush and dug around in the sandy soil. I came upon an old irrigation main, unmistakable, lined with hard smooth cobbles and dobe cement, with sluices where the water had been let out into trenches. Along these ditches I turned up some pieces of pottery, all of it broken, and arrowheads, and a very neat, well-finished stone pick-ax.

That night I didn't go back to the cabin, but took my specimens out to Blake, who was still north with the cattle. Of course, we both knew there had been Indians all over this country, but we felt sure that Indians hadn't used stone tools for a long while back. There must have been a colony of pueblo Indians here in ancient times: fixed residents, like the Taos Indians and the Hopis, not wanderers like the Navajos.

To people off alone, as we were, there is something stirring about finding evidences of human labour and care in the soil of an empty country. It comes to you as a sort of message, makes you feel differently about the ground you walk over every day. I liked the winter range better than any place I'd ever been in. I never came out of the cabin door in the morning to go after water that I didn't feel fresh delight in our snug quarters and the river and the old mesa up there, with its top burning like a bonfire. I wanted to see what it was like on the other side, and very soon I took a day off and forded the river where it was wide and shallow, north of our camp. I rode clear around the mesa, until I met the river again where it flowed under the south flank.

On that ride I got a better idea of its actual structure. All the way round were the same precipitous cliffs of hard blue rock, but in places it was mixed with a much softer stone. In these soft streaks there were deep dry watercourses which could certainly be climbed as far as they went, but nowhere did they reach to the top of the mesa. The top seemed to be one great slab of very hard rock, lying on the mixed mass of the base like the top of an old-fashioned marble table. The channels worn out by water ran for hundreds of feet up the cliffs, but always stopped under this great rimrock, which projected out over the erosions like a granite shelf. Evidently, it was because of this unbroken top layer that the butte was inaccessible. I rode back to camp that night, convinced that if we ever climbed it, we must take the route the cattle took, through the river and up the one canyon that broke down to water-level.

THREE/ We brought the bunch of cattle down to the winter range in the latter part of November. Early in December the foreman came along with generous provisions for Christmas. This time he brought with him a super-cargo, a pitiful wreck of an old man he had picked up at Tarpin, the railroad town thirty miles northeast of us, where the Sitwells bought their supplies. This old man was a castaway Englishman, Henry Atkins by name. He had been a valet, and a hospital orderly, and a cook, and for many years was a table steward on the Anchor Line. Lately he had been cooking for a sheep outfit that were grazing in the cattle country, where they weren't wanted. They had done something shady and had to get out in a hurry. They dropped old Henry at Tarpin, where he soon drank up all his wages. When Rapp picked him up there, he was living on hand-outs.

"I've told him we can't pay him anything," Rapp explained. "But if he wants to stay here and cook for you boys till I make my next trip, he'll have plenty to eat and a roof over him. He was sleeping in the livery stable in Tarpin. He says he's a good cook, and I thought he might liven things up for you at Christmas time. He won't bother you, he's not got any of the mean ways of a bum—I know a bum when I see one. Next time I come down I'll bring him some old clothes from the ranch, and you can fire him if you want to. All his baggage is that news-paper bundle, and there's nothing in it but shoes— a pair of patent leathers and a pair of sneakers. The important thing is, never, on any account, go off skylarking, you two, and leave him with the cattle. Not for an hour, mind you. He ain't strong enough, and he's got no head."

Life was a holiday for Blake and me after we got old Henry. He was a wonderful cook and a good housekeeper. He kept that cabin shining like a playhouse; used to dress it all out with piñon boughs, and trimmed the kitchen shelves with news-papers cut in fancy patterns. He had learned to make up cots when he was a hospital orderly, and he made our bunks feel like a Harvey House bed. To this day that's the best I can say for any bed. And he was such a polite, mannerly old boy; simple and kind as a child. I used to wonder how anybody so innocent and defenceless had managed to get along at all, to keep alive for nearly seventy years in as hard a world as this. Anybody could take advantage of him. He held no grudge against any of the people who had misused him. He loved to tell about the celebrated people he'd been steward to, and the liberal tips they had given him. There with us, where he couldn't get at whisky, he was a model of good behaviour. "Drink is me weakness, you might say," he occasionally remarked apologetically. He shaved every morning and was as clean as a pin. We got to be downright fond of him, and the three of us made a happy family.

Ever since we'd brought our herd down to the winter camp, the wild cattle on the mesa were more in evidence. They came down to the river to drink oftener, and loitered about, grazing in that low canyon so much that we began to call it Cow Canyon. They were fine-looking beasts, too. One could see they had good pasture up there. Henry had a theory that we ought to be able to entice them over to our side with salt. He wanted to kill one for beef-steaks. Soon after he joined us we lost two cows. Without warning they bolted into the mesa, as the foreman had said. After that we watched the herd closer; but a few days before Christmas, when Blake was off hunting and I was on duty, four fine young steers sneaked down to the water's edge through the brush, and before I knew it they were swimming the river—seemed to do it with no trouble at all. They frisked out on the other side, ambled up the canyon, and disappeared. I was furious to have them steal a march on me, and I swore to myself I'd follow them over and drive them back.

The next morning we took the herd a few miles east, to keep them out of mischief. I made some excuse to Blake, cut back to the cabin, and asked Henry to put me up a lunch. I told him my plan, but warned him not to bear tales. If I wasn't home when Blake came in at night, then he could tell him where I'd gone.

Henry went down to the river with me to watch me across. It had grown colder since morning, and looked like snow. The old man was afraid of a storm; said I might get snowed in. But I'd got my nerve up, and I didn't want to put off making a try at it. I strapped my blanket and my lunch on my shoulders, hung my boots around my neck to keep them dry, stuffed my socks inside my hat, and we waded in. My horse took the water without any fuss, though he shivered a good deal. He stepped out very carefully, and when it got too deep for him, he swam without panic. We were carried down-stream a little by the current, but I didn't have to slide off his back. He found bottom after a while, and we easily made a landing. I waved good-bye to Henry on the other side and started up the canyon, running beside my horse to get warm.

The canyon was wide at the water's edge, and though it corkscrewed back into the mesa by abrupt turns, it preserved this open, roomy character. It was, indeed, a very deep valley with gently sloping sides, rugged and rocky, but well grassed. There was a clear trail. Horses have no sense about making a trail, but you can trust cattle to find the easiest possible path and to take the lowest grades. The bluish rock and the sun-tanned grass, under the unusual purple-grey of the sky, gave the whole valley a very soft colour, lavender and pale gold, so that the occasional cedars growing beside the boulders looked black that morning. It may have been the hint of snow in the air, but it seemed to me that I had never breathed in anything that tasted so pure as the air in that valley. It made my mouth and nostrils smart like charged water, seemed to go to my head a little and produce a kind of exaltation. I kept telling myself that it was very different from the air on the other side of the river, though that was pure and uncontaminated enough.

When I had gone up this canyon for a mile or so, I came upon another, opening out to the north—a box canyon, very different in character. No gentle slope there. The walls were perpendicular, where they weren't actually overhanging, and they were anywhere from eight hundred to a thousand feet high, as we afterward found by measurement. The floor of it was a mass of huge boulders, great pieces of rock that had fallen from above ages back, and had been worn round and smooth as pebbles by the long action of water. Many of them were as big as haystacks, yet they lay piled on one another like a load of gravel. There was no footing for my horse among those smooth stones, so I hobbled him and went on alone a little way, just to see what it was like. My eyes were steadily on the ground—a slip of the foot there might cripple one.

It was such rough scrambling that I was soon in a warm sweat under my damp clothes. In stopping to take breath, I happened to glance up at the canyon wall. I wish I could tell you what I saw there, just *as* I saw it, on that first morning, through a veil of lightly falling snow. Far up above me, a thousand feet or so, set in a great cavern in the face of the cliff, I saw a little city of stone, asleep. It was as still as sculpture—and something like that. It all hung together, seemed to have a kind of composition: pale little houses of stone nestling close to one another, perched on top of each other, with flat roofs, narrow windows, straight walls, and in the middle of the group, a round tower.

It was beautifully proportioned, that tower, swelling out to a larger girth a little above the base, then growing slender again. There was something symmetrical and powerful about the swell of the masonry. The tower was the fine thing that held all the jumble of houses together and made them mean something. It was red in colour, even on that grey day. In sunlight it was the colour of winter oak-leaves. A fringe of cedars grew along the edge of the cavern, like a garden. They were the only living things. Such silence and stillness and repose—immortal repose. That village sat looking down into the canyon with the calmness of eternity. The falling snow-flakes, sprinkling the piñons, gave it a special kind of solemnity. I can't describe it. It was more like sculpture than anything else. I knew at once that I had come upon the city of some extinct civilization, hidden away in this inaccessible mesa for centuries, preserved in the dry air and almost perpetual sunlight like a fly in amber, guarded by the cliffs and the river and the desert.

As I stood looking up at it, I wondered whether I ought to tell even Blake about it; whether I ought not to go back across the river and keep that secret as the mesa had kept it. When I at last turned away, I saw still another canyon branching out of this one, and in its wall still another arch, with another group of buildings. The notion struck me like a rifle ball that this mesa had once been like a bee-hive; it was full of little cliff-hung villages, it had been the home of a powerful tribe, a particular civilization.

That night when I got home Blake was on the river-bank waiting for me. I told him I'd rather not talk about my trip until after supper,—that I was beat out. I think he'd meant to upbraid me for sneaking off, but he didn't. He seemed to realize from the first that this was a serious matter to me, and he accepted it in that way.

After supper, when we had lit our pipes, I told Blake and Henry as clearly as I could what it was like over there, and we talked it over. The town in the cliffs explained the irrigation ditches. Like all pueblo Indians, these people had had their farms away from their dwellings. For a stronghold they needed rock, and for farming, soft earth and a water main.

"And this proves," said Roddy, "that there must have been a trail into the mesa at the north end, and that they carried their harvest over by the ford. If this Cow Canyon was the only entrance, they could never have farmed down here." We agreed that he should go over on the first warm day, and try to find a trail up to the Cliff City, as we already called it.

We talked and speculated until after midnight. It was Christmas eve, and Henry said it was but right we should do something out of the ordinary. But after we went to bed, tired as I was, I was unable to sleep. I got up and dressed and put on my overcoat and slipped outside to get sight of the mesa. The wind had come up and was blowing the squall clouds across the sky. The moon was almost full, hanging directly over the mesa, which had never looked so solemn and silent to me before. I wondered how many Christmases had come and gone since that round tower was built. I had been to Acoma and the Hopi villages, but I'd never seen a tower like that one. It seemed to me to mark a difference. I felt that only a strong and aspiring people would have built it, and a people with a feeling for design. That cluster of buildings, in its arch, with the dizzy drop into empty air from its doorways and the wall of cliff above, was as clear in my mind as a picture. By closing my eyes I could see it against the dark, like a magic-lantern slide.

Blake got over the river before New Year's day, but he didn't find any way of getting from the bottom of the box canyon up into the Cliff City. He felt sure that the inhabitants of that sky village had reached it by a trail from the top of the mesa down, not from the bottom of the canyon up. He explored the branch canyons a little, and found four other villages, smaller than the first, placed in similar arches.

These arches we had often seen in other canyons. You can find them in the Grand Canyon, and all along the Rio Grande. Whenever the surface rock is much harder than the rock beneath it, the softer stone begins to crack and crumble with weather just at the line where it meets the hard rim rock. It goes on crumbling and falling away, and in time this wash-out grows to be a spacious cavern. The Cliff City sat in an unusually large cavern. We afterward found that it was three hundred and sixty feet long, and seventy feet high in the centre. The red tower was fifty feet in height.

Blake and I began to make plans. Our engagement with the Sitwell Company terminated in May. When we turned our cattle over to the foreman, we would go into the mesa with what food and tools we could carry, and try to find a trail down the north end, where we were sure there must once have been one. If we could find an easier way to get in and out of the mesa, we would devote the summer, and our winter's wages, to exploring it. From Tarpin, the nearest railroad, we could get supplies and tools, and help if we needed it. We thought we could manage to do the work ourselves if old Henry would stay with us. We didn't want to make our discovery any more public than necessary. We were reluctant to expose those silent and beautiful places to vulgar curiosity. Finally we outlined our plan to Henry, telling him we couldn't promise him regular wages.

"We won't mention it," he said, waving his hand.

"I'd ask nothing better than to share your fortunes. In me youth it was me ambition to go to Egypt and see the tombs of the Pharaohs."

"You may get a bad cold going over the river, Henry," Blake warned him. "It's bad crossing—makes you dizzy when you take to swimming. You have to keep your head."

"I was never seasick in me life," he declared, "and at that, I've helped in the cook's galley on the Anchor Line when she was fair standing on her head. You'll find me strong and active when I'm once broke into the work. I come of an enduring family, though, to be sure, I've abused me constitution somewhat."

Henry liked to talk about his family, and the work they'd done, and the great age to which they lived, and the brandy puddings his mother made. "Eighteen we was in all, when we sat down at table," he would often say with his thin, apologetic smile. "Mother and father, and ten living, and four dead, and two still-born." Roddy and I used to strain our imagination trying to visualize such a family dinner party.

Everything worked out well for us. The foreman showed so much interest in our plans that we told him everything. He insisted that we should stay on at the winter camp as long as we needed a home base, and use up whatever supplies were left. When he paid us off, he sold us our two horses at a very reasonable figure.

FOUR /   Blake and I got over to the mesa together for the first time early in May. We carried with us all the food we could, and an ax and spade. It took us several days to find a trail leading from the bottom of the box canyon up to the Cliff City. There were gaps in it; it was broken by ledges too steep for a man to climb. Lying beside one of these, we found an old dried cedar trunk, with toe-notches cut in it. That was a plain suggestion. We felled some trees and threw them up over the gaps in the path. Toward the end of the week, when our provisions were getting low, we made the last lap in our climb, and stepped upon the ledge that was the floor of the Cliff City.

In front of the cluster of buildings, there was an open space, like a court-yard. Along the outer edge of this yard ran a low stone wall. In some places the wall had fallen away from the weather, but the buildings themselves sat so far back under the rim rock that the rain had never beat on them. In thunderstorms I've seen the water come down in sheets over the face of that cavern without a drop touching the village.

The court-yard was not choked by vegetation, for there was no soil. It was bare rock, with a few old, flat-topped cedars growing out of the cracks, and a little pale grass. But everything seemed open and clean, and the stones, I remember, were warm to the touch, smooth and pleasant to feel.

The outer walls of the houses were intact, except where sometimes an outjutting corner had crumbled. They were made of dressed stones, plastered inside and out with 'dobe, and were tinted in light colours, pink and pale yellow and tan. Here and there a cedar log in the ceiling had given way and let the second-story chamber down into the first; except for that, there was little rubbish or disorder. As Blake remarked, wind and sun are good housekeepers.

This village had never been sacked by an enemy, certainly. Inside the little rooms water jars and bowls stood about unbroken, and yucca-fibre mats were on the floors.

We could give only a hurried look over the place, as our food was exhausted, and we had to get back over the river before dark. We went about softly, tried not to disturb anything—even the silence. Besides the tower, there seemed to be about thirty little separate dwellings. Behind the cluster of houses was a kind of back court-yard, running from end to end of the cavern; a long, low, twilit space that got gradually lower toward the back until the rim rock met the floor of the cavern, exactly like the sloping roof of an attic. There was perpetual twilight back there, cool, shadowy, very grateful after the blazing sun in the front court-yard. When we entered it we heard a soft trickling sound, and we came upon a spring that welled out of the rock into a stone basin and then ran off through a cobble-lined gutter and dripped down the cliffs. I've never anywhere tasted water like it; as cold as ice, and so pure. Long afterward Father Duchene came out to spend a week with us on the mesa; he always carried a small drinking-glass with him, and he used to fill it at the spring and take it out into the sunlight. The water looked like liquid crystal, absolutely colourless, without the slight brownish or greenish tint that water nearly always has. It threw off the sunlight like a diamond.

Beside this spring stood some of the most beautifully shaped water jars we ever found—I gave Mrs. St. Peter one of them—standing there just as if they'd been left yesterday. In the back court we found a great many things besides jars and bowls: a row of grinding-stones, and several clay ovens, very much like those the Mexicans use to-day. There were charred bones and charcoal, and the roof was thick with soot all the way along. It was evidently a kind of common kitchen, where they roasted and baked and probably gossiped. There were corncobs everywhere, and ears of corn with the kernels still on them—little, like popcorn. We found dried beans, too, and strings of pumpkin seeds, and plum seeds, and a cupboard full of little implements made of turkey bones.

Late that afternoon Roddy and I crossed the river and got back to our cabin to rest for a few days.

The second time we went over, we found a long winding trail leading from the Cliff City up to the top of the mesa—a narrow path worn deep into the stone ledges that overhung the village, then running back into the wood of stunted piñons on the summit. Following this to the north end of the mesa, we found what was left of an old road down to the plain. But making this road passable was a matter of weeks, and we had to get workmen and tools from Tarpin. It was a narrow foot-path, barely wide enough for a sure-footed mule, and it wound down through Black Canyon, dropping in loops along the face of terrifying cliffs. About a hundred feet above the river, it ended—broke right off into the air. A wall of rock had fallen away there, probably from a landslide. That last piece of road cost us three weeks' hard work, and most of our winter's wages. We kept the workmen on long enough to build us a tight log cabin on the mesa top, a little way back from the ledge that hung over the Cliff City.

While we were engaged in road-building, we made a short cut from our cabin down to the Cliff City and Cow Canyon. Just over the Cliff City, there was a crack in the ledge, a sort of manhole, and in this we hung a ladder of pine-trunks spliced together with light chains, leaving the branch forks for foot-holds. By climbing down this ladder we saved about two miles of winding trail, and dropped almost directly into Cow Canyon, where we meant always to leave one of the horses grazing. Taking this route, we

could at any time make a quick exit from the mesa—
we were used to swimming the river now, and in
summer our wet clothes dried very quickly.

Bill Hook, the liveryman at Tarpin, who'd sheltered old Henry when he was down and out, proved
a good friend to us. He got our workmen back and
forth for us, brought our supplies up on to the mesa
on his pack-mules, and when one of us had to stay in
town overnight he let us sleep in his hay barn to
save a hotel bill. He knew our expenses were heavy,
and did everything for us at a bottom price.

By the first of July our money was nearly gone,
but we had our road made, and our cabin built on
top of the mesa. We brought old Henry up by the
new horse-trail and began housekeeping. We were
now ready for what we called excavating. We built
wide shelves all around our sleeping-room, and there
we put the smaller articles we found in the Cliff City.
We numbered each specimen, and in my day-book I
wrote down just where and in what condition we had
found it, and what we thought it had been used for.
I'd got a merchant's ledger in Tarpin, and every night
after supper, while Roddy read the newspapers, I sat
down at the kitchen table and wrote up an account
of the day's work.

Henry, besides doing the housekeeping, was very
eager to help us in the "rew-ins," as he called them.
He was more patient than we, and would dig with
his fingers half a day to get a pot out of a rubbish
pile without breaking it. After all, the old man had
a wider knowledge of the world than either of us,
and it often came in handy. When we were working in a pale pink house, with two stories, and a
sort of balcony before the upper windows, we came
on a closet in the wall of the upstairs room; in this
were a number of curious things, among them a deer-
skin bag full of little tools. Henry said at once they

were surgical instruments; a stone lancet, a bunch of fine bone needles, wooden forceps, and a catheter.

One thing we knew about these people; they hadn't built their town in a hurry. Everything proved their patience and deliberation. The cedar joists had been felled with stone axes and rubbed smooth with sand. The little poles that lay across them and held up the clay floor of the chamber above, were smoothly polished. The door lintels were carefully fitted (the doors were stone slabs held in place by wooden bars fitted into hasps). The clay dressing that covered the stone walls was tinted, and some of the chambers were frescoed in geometrical patterns, one colour laid on another. In one room was a painted border, little tents, like Indian tepees, in brilliant red.

But the really splendid thing about our city, the thing that made it delightful to work there, and must have made it delightful to live there, was the setting. The town hung like a bird's nest in the cliff, looking off into the box canyon below, and beyond into the wide valley we called Cow Canyon, facing an ocean of clear air. A people who had the hardihood to build there, and who lived day after day looking down upon such grandeur, who came and went by those hazardous trails, must have been, as we often told each other, a fine people. But what had become of them? What catastrophe had overwhelmed them?

They hadn't moved away, for they had taken none of their belongings, not even their clothes. Oh, yes, we found clothes; yucca moccasins, and what seemed like cotton cloth, woven in black and white. Never any wool, but sheepskins tanned with the fleece on them. They may have been mountain sheep; the mesa was full of them. We talked of shooting one for meat, but we never did. When a mountain sheep comes out on a ledge hundreds of feet above you, with his trumpet horns, there's something noble about him—he looks like a priest. We didn't want to shoot at them and make them shy. We liked to see them. We shot a wild cow when we wanted fresh meat.

At last we came upon one of the original inhabitants—not a skeleton, but a dried human body, a woman. She was not in the Cliff City; we found her in a little group of houses stuck up in a high arch we called the Eagle's Nest. She was lying on a yucca mat, partly covered with rags, and she had dried into a mummy in that water-drinking air. We thought she had been murdered; there was a great wound in her side, the ribs stuck out through the dried flesh. Her mouth was open as if she were screaming, and her face, through all those years, had kept a look of terrible agony. Part of the nose was gone, but she had plenty of teeth, not one missing, and a great deal of coarse black hair. Her teeth were even and white, and so little worn that we thought she must have been a young woman. Henry named her Mother Eve, and we called her that. We put her in a blanket and let her down with great care, and kept her in a chamber in the Cliff City.

Yes, we found three other bodies, but afterward. One day, working in the Cliff City, we came upon a stone slab at one end of the cavern, that seemed to lead straight into the rock. It was set in cement, and when we loosened it we found it opened into a small, dark chamber. In this there had been a platform, of fine cedar poles laid side by side, but it had crumbled. In the wreckage were three bodies, one man and two women, wrapped in yucca-fibre, all in the same posture and apparently prepared for burial. They were the bodies of old people. We believed they were among the aged who were left behind when the tribe went down to live on their farms in the summer season; that they had died in the absence of the villagers, and were put into this mortuary chamber to await the return of the tribe, when they would have their funeral rites. Probably these people burned their dead. Of course an archæologist could have told a great deal about that civilization from those bodies. But they never got to an archæologist—at least, not on this side of the world.

FIVE/ The first of August came, and everything was going well with us. We hadn't met with any bad luck, and though we had very little money left, there was Blake's untouched savings account in the bank at Pardee, and we had plenty of credit in Tarpin. The merchants there took an interest and were friendly. But the little new moon, that looked so innocent, brought us trouble. We lost old Henry, and in a terrible way. From the first we'd been a little bothered by rattlesnakes—you generally find them about old stone quarries and old masonry. We had got them pretty well cleared out of the Cliff City, hadn't seen one there for weeks. But one Sunday we took Henry and went on an exploring expedition at the north end of the mesa, along Black Canyon. We caught sight of a little bunch of ruins we'd never noticed before, and made a foolhardy scramble to get up to them. We almost made it, and then there was a stretch of rock wall so smooth we couldn't climb it without a ladder. I was the tallest of the three, and Henry was the lightest; he thought he could get up there if he stood on my shoulders. He was standing on my back, his head just above the floor of the cavern, groping for something to hoist himself by, when a snake struck him from the ledge—struck him square in the forehead. It happened in a flash. He came down and brought the snake with him. By the time we picked him up and turned him over, his face had begun to swell. In ten minutes it was purple, and he was so crazy it took the two of us to hold him and keep him from jumping down the chasm. He was struck so near the brain that there was nothing to do. It lasted nearly two hours. Then we carried him home. Roddy dropped down the ladder into Cow Canyon, caught his horse, and rode into Tarpin for the coroner. Father Duchene was preaching there at the mission church that Sunday, and came back with him.

We buried Henry on the mesa. Father Duchene stayed on with us a week to keep us company. We were so cut up that we were almost ready to quit. But he had been planning to come out to see our find for a long while, and he got our minds off our trouble. He worked hard every day. He went over everything we'd done, and examined everything minutely: the pottery, cloth, stone implements, and the remains of food. He measured the heads of the mummies and declared they had good skulls. He cut down one of the old cedars that grew exactly in the middle of the deep trail worn in the stone, and counted the rings under his pocket microscope. You couldn't count them with the unassisted eye, for growing out of a tiny crevice in the rock as that tree did, the increase of each year was so scant that the rings were invisible except with a glass. The tree he cut down registered three hundred and thirty-six years' growth, and it could have begun to grow in that well-worn path only after human feet had ceased to come and go there.

Why had they ceased? That question puzzled him, too. Smallpox, any epidemic, would have left unburied bodies. Father Duchene suggested what Dr. Ripley, in Washington, afterward surmised: that the tribe had been exterminated, not here in their stronghold, but in their summer camp, down among the farms across the river. Father Duchene had been among the Indians nearly twenty years then, he had seventeen Indian pueblos in his parish, and he spoke several Indian dialects. He was able to explain the use of many of the implements we found, especially those used in religious ceremonies. The night before he left us, he summed up the results of his week's study, something like this:

"The two square towers on the mesa top, to which you have given little attention, were unquestionably granaries. Under the stones and earth fallen from the walls, there is a quantity of dried corn on the ear. Not a great harvest, for life must have come to an end here in the summer, when the new crop was not yet garnered and the last year's grain was getting low. The semicircular ridge on the mesa top, which you can see distinctly among the piñons when the sun is low and brings it into high relief, is the buried wall of an amphitheatre, where probably religious exercises and games took place. I advise you not to dig into it. It is probably the most important thing here, and should be left for scholars to excavate.

"The tower you so much admire in the cliff village may have been a watch tower, as you think, but from the curious placing of those narrow slits, like windows, I believe it was used for astronomical observations. I am inclined to think that your tribe were a superior people. Perhaps they were not so when they first came upon this mesa, but in an orderly and secure life they developed considerably the arts of peace. There is evidence on every hand that they lived for something more than food and shelter. They had an appreciation of comfort, and went even further than that. Their life, compared to that of our roving Navajos, must have been quite complex. There is unquestionably a distinct feeling for design in what you call the Cliff City. Buildings are not grouped like that by pure accident, though convenience probably

45

had much to do with it. Convenience often dictates very sound design.

"The workmanship on both the wood and stone of the dwellings is good. The shapes and decoration of the water jars and food bowls is better than in any of the existing pueblos I know, better even than the pottery made at Acoma. I have seen a collection of early pottery from the island of Crete. Many of the geometrical decorations on these jars are not only similar, but, if my memory is trustworthy, identical.

"I see your tribe as a provident, rather thoughtful people, who made their livelihood secure by raising crops and fowl—the great number of turkey bones and feathers are evidence that they had domesticated the wild turkey. With grain in their storerooms, and mountain sheep and deer for their quarry, they rose gradually from the condition of savagery. With the proper variation of meat and vegetable diet, they developed physically and improved in the primitive arts. They had looms and mills, and experimented with dyes. At the same time, they possibly declined in the arts of war, in brute strength and ferocity.

"I see them here, isolated, cut off from other tribes, working out their destiny, making their mesa more and more worthy to be a home for man, purifying life by religious ceremonies and observances, caring respectfully for their dead, protecting the children, doubtless entertaining some feelings of affection and sentiment for this stronghold where they were at once so safe and so comfortable, where they had practically overcome the worst hardships that primitive man had to fear. They were, perhaps, too far advanced for their time and environment.

"They were probably wiped out, utterly exterminated, by some roving Indian tribe without culture or domestic virtues, some horde that fell upon them in their summer camp and destroyed them for their hides and clothing and weapons, or from mere love of slaughter. I feel sure that these brutal invaders never even learned of the existence of this mesa, honeycombed with habitations. If they had come here, they would have destroyed. They killed and went their way.

"What I cannot understand is why you have not found more human remains. The three bodies you found in the mortuary chamber were prepared for burial by the old people who were left behind. But what of the last survivors? It is possible that when autumn wore on, and no one returned from the farms, the aged banded together, went in search of their people, and perished in the plain.

"Like you, I feel a reverence for this place. Wherever humanity has made that hardest of all starts and lifted itself out of mere brutality, is a sacred spot. Your people were cut off here without the influence of example or emulation, with no incentive but some natural yearning for order and security. They built themselves into this mesa and humanized it."

Father Duchene warmly agreed with Blake that I ought to go to Washington and make some report to the Government, so that the proper specialists would be sent out to study the remains we had found.

"You must go to the Director of the Smithsonian Institution," he said. "He will send us an archæologist who will interpret all that is obscure to us. He will revive this civilization in a scholarly work. It may be that you will have thrown light on some important points in the history of your country."

After he left us, Blake and I began to make definite plans for my trip to Washington. Blake was to work on the railroad that winter and save as much money as possible. The expense of my journey would be paid out of what we called the jackpot account, in the bank at Pardee. All our further expenses on the mesa would be paid by the Government. Roddy often hinted that we would get a substantial reward of some kind. When we broke or lost anything at our work, he used to smile and say: "Never mind. I guess our Uncle Sam will make that good to us."

We had a beautiful autumn that year, soft, sunny, like a dream. Even up there in the air we had so little wind that the gold hung on the poplars and quaking aspens late in November. We stayed out on the mesa until after Christmas. We wanted our archæologist, when he came, to find everything in good order. We cleared up any litter we'd made in digging things out, stored all the specimens, even the mummies, in our cabin, and padlocked the doors and windows before we left it. I had written up my day-book carefully to the very end, had even written out some of Father Duchene's deductions. This book I left in concealment on the mesa. I climbed up to the Eagle's Nest in which we had found the mummy of the murdered woman we called Mother Eve, where I had noticed a particularly neat little cupboard in the wall. I put my book in this niche and sealed it up with cement. Mother Eve had greatly interested Father Duchene, by the way. He laughed and said she was well named. He didn't believe her death could throw any light on the destruction of her people. "I seem to smell," he said slyly, "a personal tragedy. Perhaps when the tribe went down to the summer camp, our lady was sick and would not go. Perhaps her husband thought it worth while to return unannounced from the farms some night, and found her in improper company. The young man may have escaped. In primitive society the husband is allowed to punish an unfaithful wife with death."

When the first snow began to fly, we said good-bye to our mesa and rode into Tarpin. It took several days to outfit me for my journey to Washington. We bought a trunk (I'd never owned one in my life), and a supply of white shirts, an overcoat that was as heavy as lead and just about as cold, and two suits of clothes. That conscienceless trader worked off on me a clawhammer coat he must have had in stock for twenty years. He easily persuaded Roddy that it was the proper thing for dress occasions. I think Roddy expected that I would be received by ambassadors— perhaps I did.

Roddy drew six hundred dollars out of the bank to stake me, and bought my ticket and Pullman through to Washington. He went to the station with me the morning I left, and a hard handshake was good-bye.

For a long while after my train pulled out, I could see our mesa bulking up blue on the sky-line. I hated to leave it, but I reflected that it had taken care of itself without me for a good many hundred years. When I saw it again, I told myself, I would have done my duty by it; I would bring back with me men who would understand it, who would appreciate it and dig out all its secrets.

SIX / I got off the train, just behind the Capitol building, one cold bright January morning. I stood for a long while watching the white dome against a flashing blue sky, with a very religious feeling. After I had walked about a little and seen the parks, so green though it was winter, and the Treasury building, and the War and Navy, I decided to put off my business for a little and give myself a week to enjoy the city. That was the most sensible thing I did while I was there. For that week I was wonderfully happy.

My sightseeing over, I got to work. First I went

to see the Representative from our district, to ask for letters of introduction. He was cordial enough, but he gave me bad advice. He was very positive that I ought to report to the Indian Commission, and gave me a letter to the Commissioner. The Commissioner was out of town, and I wasted three days waiting about his office, being questioned by clerks and secretaries. They were not very busy, and seemed to find me entertaining. I thought they were interested in my mission, and interest was what I wanted to arouse. I didn't know how influential these people might be— they talked as if they had great authority. I had brought along in my telescope bag some good pieces of pottery—not the best, I was afraid of accident, but some that were representative—and all the photographs Blake and I had taken. We had only a small kodak, and these pictures didn't make much show,— looked, indeed, like grubby little 'dobe ruins such as one can find almost anywhere. They gave no idea of the beauty and vastness of the setting. The clerks at the Indian Commission seemed very curious about everything and made me talk a lot. I was green and didn't know any better. But when one of the fellows there tried to get me to give him my best bowl for his cigarette ashes, I began to suspect the nature of their interest.

At last the Commissioner returned, but he had pressing engagements, and I hung around several days more before he would see me. After questioning me for about half an hour, he told me that his business was with living Indians, not dead ones, and that his office should have informed me of that in the beginning. He advised me to go back to our Congressman and get a letter to the Smithsonian Institution. I packed up my pottery and got out of the place, feeling pretty sore. The head clerk followed me down the corridor and asked me what I'd take for that little bowl he'd taken a fancy to. He said it had no market value, I'd find Washington full of such things; there were cases of them in the cellar at the Smithsonian that they'd never taken the trouble to unpack, hadn't any place to put them.

I went back to my Congressman. This time he wasn't so friendly as before, but he gave me a letter to the Smithsonian. There I went through the same experience. The Director couldn't be seen except by appointment, and his secretary had to be convinced that your business was important before he would give you an appointment with his chief. After the first morning I found it difficult to see even the secretary. He was always engaged. I was told to take a seat and wait, but when he was disengaged he was hurrying off to luncheon. I would sit there all morning with a group of unfortunate people: girls who wanted to get typewriting to do, nice polite old men who wanted to be taken out on surveys and expeditions next summer. The secretary would at last come out with his overcoat on, and would hurry through the waiting-room reading a letter or a report, without looking up.

The office assistants cheered me along, and I kept this up for some days, sitting all morning in that room, studying the patterns of the rugs, and the shoes of the patient waiters who came as regularly as I. One day after the secretary had gone out, his stenographer, a nice little Virginia girl, came and sat down in an empty chair next to mine and began talking to me. She wasn't pretty, but her kind eyes and soft Southern voice took hold of me at once. She wanted to know what I had in my telescope, and why I was there, and where I came from, and all about it. Nearly everyone else had gone out to lunch—that seemed to be the one thing they did regularly in Washington —and we had the waiting-room to ourselves. I talked to her a good deal. Her name was Virginia Ward. She was a tiny little thing, but she had lovely eyes and such gentle ways. She seemed indignant that I had been put off so long after having come so far.

"Now you just let me fix it up for you," she said at last. "Mr. Wagner is bothered by a great many foolish people who waste his time, and he is suspicious. The best way will be for you to invite him to lunch with you. I'll arrange it. I keep a list of his appointments, and I know he is not engaged for luncheon to-morrow. I'll tell him that he is to lunch with a nice boy who has come all the way from New Mexico to inform the Department about an important discovery. I'll tell him to meet you at the Shoreham, at one. That's expensive, but it would do no good to invite him to a cheap place. And, remember, you must ask him to order the luncheon. It will maybe cost you ten dollars, but it will get you somewhere."

I felt grateful to the nice little thing,—she wasn't older than I. I begged her wouldn't she please come to lunch with me herself to-day, and talk to me.

"Oh, no!" she said, blushing red as a poppy. "Why, I'm afraid you think—"

I told her I didn't think anything but how nice she was to me, and how lonesome I was. She went with me, but she wouldn't go to any swell place. She told me a great many useful things.

"If you want to get attention from anybody in Washin'ton," she said, "ask them to lunch. People here will do almost anything for a good lunch."

"But the Director of the Smithsonian, for instance," I said, "surely you don't mean that the high-up ones like that—? Why would he want to bother with a cow-puncher from New Mexico, when he can lunch with scientists and ambassadors?"

She had a pretty little fluttery Southern laugh. "You just name a hotel like the Shoreham to the

Director, and try it! There has to be somebody to pay for a lunch, and the scientists and ambassadors don't do that when they can avoid it. He'd accept your invitation, and the next time he went to dine with the Secretary of State he'd make a nice little story of it, and paint you up so pretty you'd hardly know yourself."

When I asked her whether I'd better take my pottery—it was there under the table between us—to the Shoreham to show Mr. Wagner, she tittered again. "I wouldn't bother. If you show him enough of the Shoreham pottery, that will be more effective."

The next morning, when the secretary arrived at his office, he stopped by my chair and said he understood he had an engagement with me for one o'clock. That was a good idea, he added: his mind was freer when he was away from office routine.

I had been in Washington twenty-two days when I took the secretary out to lunch. It was an excellent lunch. We had a bottle of Château d'Yquem. I'd never heard of such a wine before, but I remember it because it cost five dollars. I drank only one glass, and that pleased him too, for he drank the rest. Though he was friendly and talked a great deal, my heart sank lower, for he wouldn't let me explain my mission to him at all. He kept telling me that he knew all about the Southwest. He had been sent by the Smithsonian to conduct parties of European archæologists through all the show places, Frijoles and Canyon de Chelly, and Taos and the Hopi pueblos. When some Austrian Archduke had gone to hunt in the Pecos range, he had been sent by his chief and the German ambassador to manage the tour, and he had done it with such success that both he and the Director were given decorations from the Austrian Crown, in recognition of his services. Then I had to listen to a long story about how well he was treated by the Archduke when he went to Vienna with his chief the following summer. I had to hear about balls and receptions, and the names and titles of all the poeple he had met at the Duke's country estate. I was amazed and ashamed that a man of fifty, a man of the world, a scholar with ever so many degrees, should find it worth his while to show off before a boy, and a boy of such humble pretensions, who didn't know how to eat the *hors d'œuvres* any more than if an assortment of cocoanuts had been set before him with no hammer.

Imagine my astonishment when, as he was drinking his liqueur, he said carelessly: "By the way, I was successful in arranging an interview with the Director for you. He will see you at four o'clock on Monday."

That was Thursday. I spent the time between then and Monday trying to find out something more about the kind of people I had come among. I persuaded Virginia Ward to go to the theatre with me, and she told me that it always took a long while to get anything through with the Director, that I mustn't lose heart, and she would always be glad to cheer me up. She lived with her mother, a widow lady, and they had me come to dinner and were very nice to me.

All this time I was living with a young married couple who interested me very much, for they were unlike any people I had ever known. The husband was "in office," as they say there, he had some position in the War Department. How it did use to depress me to see all the hundreds of clerks come pouring out of that building at sunset! Their lives seemed to me so petty, so slavish. The couple I lived with gave me a prejudice against that kind of life. I couldn't help knowing a good deal about their affairs. They had only a small flat, and rented me one room of it, so I was very much in their confidence and couldn't help overhearing. They asked me not to mention the fact that I paid rent, as they had told their friends I was making them a visit. It was like that in everything; they spent their lives trying to keep up appearances, and to make his salary do more than it could. When they weren't discussing where she should go in the summer, they talked about the promotions in his department; how much the other clerks got and how they spent it, how many new dresses their wives had. And there was always a struggle going on for an invitation to a dinner or a reception, or even a tea-party. When once they got the invitation they had been scheming for, then came the terrible question of what Mrs. Bixby should wear.

The Secretary of War gave a reception; there was to be dancing and a great showing of foreign uniforms. The Bixbys were in painful suspense until they got a card. Then for a week they talked about nothing but what Mrs. Bixby was going to wear. They decided that for such an occasion she must have a new dress. Bixby borrowed twenty-five dollars from me, and took his lunch hour to go shopping with his wife and choose the satin. That seemed to me very strange. In New Mexico the Indian boys sometimes went to a trader's with their wives and bought shawls or calico, and we thought it rather contemptible. On the night of the reception the Bixbys set off gaily in a cab; the dress they considered a great success. But they had bad luck. Somebody spilt claret-cup on Mrs. Bixby's skirt before the evening was half over, and when they got home that night I heard her weeping and reproaching him for having been so upset about it, and looking at nothing but her ruined dress all evening. She said he cried out when it happened. I don't doubt it.

Every cab, every party, was more than they could afford. If he lost an umbrella, it was a real misfortune. He wasn't lazy, he wasn't a fool, and he meant to be honest; but he was intimidated by that miserable sort of departmental life. He didn't know anything else. He thought working in a store or a bank not respectable. Living with the Bixbys gave me a kind of low-spiritedness I had never known before. During my days of waiting for appointments, I used to walk for hours around the fence that shuts in the White House grounds, and watch the Washington monument colour with those beautiful sunsets, until the time when all the clerks streamed out of the Treasury building and the War and Navy. Thousands of them, all more or less like the couple I lived with. They seemed to me like people in slavery, who ought to be free. I remember the city chiefly by those beautiful, hazy, sad sunsets, white columns and green shrubbery, and the monument shaft still pink while the stars were coming out.

I got my interview with the Director of the Smithsonian at last. He gave me his attention, he was interested. He told me to come again in three days and meet Dr. Ripley, who was the authority on prehistoric Indian remains and had excavated a lot of them. Then came an exciting and rather encouraging time for me. Dr. Ripley asked the right sort of questions, and evidently knew his business. He said he'd like to take the first train down to my mesa. But it required money to excavate, and he had none. There was a bill up before Congress for an appropriation. We'd have to wait. I must use my influence with my Representative. He took my pottery to study it. (I never got it back, by the way.) There was a Dr. Fox, connected with the Smithsonian, who was also interested. They told me a good many things I wanted to know, and kept me dangling about the office. Of course they were very kind to take so much trouble with a green boy. But I soon found that the Director and all his staff had one interest which dwarfed every other. There was to be an International Exposition of some sort in Europe the following summer, and they were all pulling strings to get appointed on juries or sent to international congresses—appointments that would pay their expenses abroad, and give them a salary in addition. There was, indeed, a bill before Congress for appropriations for the Smithsonian; but there was also a bill for Exposition appropriations, and that was the one they were really pushing. They kept me hanging on through March and April, but in the end it came to nothing. Dr. Ripley told me he was sorry, but the sum Congress had allowed the Smithsonian wouldn't cover an expedition to the Southwest.

Virginia Ward, who had been so kind to me, went out to lunch with me that day, and admitted I had been let down. She was almost as much disappointed as I. She said the only thing Dr. Ripley really cared about was getting a free trip to Europe and acting on a jury, and maybe getting a decoration. "And that's what the Director wants, too," she said. "They don't care much about dead and gone Indians. What they do care about is going to Paris, and getting another ribbon on their coats."

The only other person besides Virginia who was genuinely concerned about my affair was a young Frenchman, a lieutenant attached to the French Embassy, who came to the Smithsonian often on business connected with this same International Exposition. He was nice and polite to Virginia, and she introduced him to me. We used to walk down along the Potomac together. He studied my photographs and asked me such intelligent questions about everything that it was a pleasure to talk to him. He had a fine attitude about it all; he was thoughtful, critical, and respectful. I feel sure he'd have gone back to New Mexico with me if he'd had the money. He was even poorer than I.

I was utterly ashamed to go home to Roddy, dead broke after all the money I'd spent, and without a thing to show for it. I hung on in Washington through May, trying to get a job of some sort, to at least earn my fare home. My letters to Blake had been pretty blue for some time back. If I'd been sensible, I'd have kept my troubles to myself. He was easily discouraged, and I knew that. At last I had to write him for money to go home. It was slow in coming, and I began to telegraph. I left Washington at last, wiser than I came. I had no plans, I wanted nothing but to get back to the mesa and live a free life and breathe free air, and never, never again to see hundreds of little black-coated men pouring out of white buildings. Queer, how much more depressing they are than workmen coming out of a factory.

I was terribly disappointed when I got off the train at Tarpin and Roddy wasn't at the station to meet me. It was late in the afternoon, almost dark, and I went straight to the livery stable to ask Bill Hook for news of Blake. Hook, you remember, had done all our hauling for us, and had been a good friend. He gave me a glad hand and said Blake was out on the mesa.

"I expect maybe he's had his feelings hurt here. He's been shy of this town lately. You see, Tom, folks weren't bothered none about that mesa so long as you fellows were playing Robinson Crusoe out there, digging up curios. But when it leaked out that Blake had got a lot of money for your stuff, then they begun to feel jealous—said them ruins didn't belong to Blake any more than to anybody else. It'll blow over in time; people are always like that when money changes hands. But right now there's a good deal of bad feeling."

I told him I didn't know what he was talking about.

"You mean you ain't heard about the German, Fechtig? Well, Rodney's got some surprise waiting for you! Why, he's had the damnedest luck! He's cleaned up a neat little pile on your stuff."

I begged him to tell me what stuff he meant.

"Why, your curios. This German, Fechtig, come along; he'd been buying up a lot of Indian things out here, and he bought your whole outfit and paid four thousand dollars down for it. The transaction made quite a stir here in Tarpin. I'm not kicking. I made a good thing out of it. My mules were busy three weeks packing the stuff out of there on their backs, and I held the Dutchman up for a fancy price. He had packing cases made at the wagon shop and took 'em up to the mesa full of straw and saw-dust, and packed the curios out there. I lost one of my mules, too. You remember Jenny? Well, they were leading her down with a big box on her, and right there where the trail runs so narrow around a bump in the cliff above Black Canyon, she lost her balance and fell clean to the bottom, her load on her. Pretty near a thousand feet, I guess. We never went down to hold a post-mortem, but Fechtig paid for her like a gentleman."

I remember I sat down on the sofa in Hook's office because I couldn't stand up any longer, and the smell of the horse blankets began to make me deathly sick. In a minute I went over, like a girl in a novel. Hook pulled me out on the sidewalk and gave me some whisky out of his pocket flask.

When I felt better I asked him how long this German had been gone, and what he had done with the things.

"Oh, he cleared out three weeks ago. He didn't

59

waste no time. He treated everybody well, though; nobody's sore at him. It's your partner they're turned against. Fechtig took the stuff right along with him, chartered a freight car, and travelled in the car with it. I reckon it's on the water by now. He took it straight through into Old Mexico, and was to load it on a French boat. Seems he was afraid of having trouble getting curiosities out of the United States ports. You know you can take anything out of the City of Mexico."

I had heard all I wanted to hear. I went to the hotel, got a room, and lay down without undressing to wait for daylight. Hook was to drive me and my trunk out to the mesa early the next morning. All I'd been through in Washington was nothing to what I went through that night. I thought Blake must have lost his mind. I didn't for a minute believe he'd meant to sell me out, but I cursed his stupidity and presumption. I had never told him just how I felt about those things we'd dug out together, it was the kind of thing one doesn't talk about directly. But he must have known; he couldn't have lived with me all summer and fall without knowing. And yet, until that night, I had never known myself that I cared more about them than about anything else in the world.

At the first blink of daylight I jumped up from my damnable bed and went round to the stable to rout Hook out of his bunk. We had breakfast and got out of town with his best team. On the way to the mesa we had a break-down, one of the old dry wheels smashed to splinters. Hook had to unhitch and ride back to Tarpin and get another. Everything took an unreasonably long time, and the afternoon was half gone when he put me and my trunk down at the foot of the Black Canyon trail. Every inch of that trail was dear to me, every delicate curve about the old piñon roots, every chancy track along the face of the cliffs, and the deep windings back into shrubbery and safety. The wild-currant bushes were in bloom, and where the path climbed the side of a narrow ravine, the scent of them in the sun was so heavy that it made me soft, made me want to lie down and sleep. I wanted to see and touch everything, like home-sick children when they come home.

When I pulled out on top of the mesa, the rays of sunlight fell slantingly through the little twisted piñons,—the light was all in between them, as red as a daylight fire, they fairly swam in it. Once again I had that glorious feeling that I've never had anywhere else, the feeling of being *on the mesa*, in a world above the world. And the air, my God, what air!—Soft, tingling, gold, hot with an edge of chill on it, full of the smell of piñons—it was like breathing the sun, breathing the colour of the sky. Down there behind me was the plain, already streaked with shadow, violet and purple and burnt orange until it met the horizon. Before me was the flat mesa top, thinly sprinkled with old cedars that were not much taller than I, though their twisted trunks were almost as thick as my body. I struck off across it, my long black shadow going ahead.

I made straight for the cabin, it was about three miles from the spot where the trail emerged at the top. I saw smoke rising before I could see the hut itself. Blake was in the doorway when I got there. I didn't look at his face, but I could feel that he looked at mine.

"Don't say anything, Tom. Don't rip me up until you hear all about it," he said as I came toward him.

"I've heard enough to about do for me," I blurted out. "What made you do it, Blake? What made you do it?"

"It was a chance in a million, boy. There wasn't any time to consult you. There's only one man in thousands that wants to buy relics and pay real money for them. I could see how your Washington campaign was coming out. I know you'd thought about big figures, so had I. But that was all a pipe dream. Four thousand's not so bad, you don't pick it up every day. And he bore all the expenses. Why, it was a terrible expensive job, getting all that frail stuff out of here. Who else would have bought it, I want to know? We'd have had to pack it around at Harvey Houses, selling it at a dollar a bowl, like the poor Indians do. I took the best chance going, for both of us, Tom."

I didn't say anything, because there was too much to say. I stood outside the cabin until the gold light went blue and a few stars came out, hardly brighter than the bright sky they twinkled in, and the swallows came flying over us, on their way to their nests in the cliffs. It was the time of day when everything goes home. From habit and from weariness I went in through the door. The kitchen table was spread for supper, I could smell a rabbit stew cooking on the stove. Blake lit the lantern and begged me to eat my supper. I didn't go into the bunk-room, for I knew the shelves in there were empty. I heard Blake talking to me as you hear people talking when you are asleep.

"Who else would have bought them?" he kept saying. "Folks make a lot of fuss over such things, but they don't want to pay good money for them."

When I at last told him that such a thing as selling them had never entered my head, I'm sure he thought I was lying. He reminded me about how we used to talk of getting big money from the Government.

I admitted I'd hoped we'd be paid for our work, and maybe get a bonus of some kind, for our discovery. "But I never thought of selling them, because they weren't mine to sell—nor yours! They belonged to this country, to the State, and to all the people. They belonged to boys like you and me, that have no other ancestors to inherit from. You've gone and sold them to a country that's got plenty of relics of its own. You've gone and sold your country's secrets, like Dreyfus."

"That man was innocent. It was a frame-up," Blake murmured. It was a point he would never pass up.

"Whether he's guilty or not, you are! If there was only anybody in Washington I could telegraph to, and have that German held up at the port!"

"That's just it. If there was anybody in Washington that cared a damn, I wouldn't have sold 'em. But you pretty well found out there ain't."

"We could have kept them, then," I told him. "I've got a strong back. I'm not so poor that I have to sell the pots and pans that belonged to my poor grandmothers a thousand years ago. I made all my plans on the train, coming back." (It was a lie, I hadn't.) "I meant to get a job on the railroad and keep our find right here, and come back to it when I had a lay-off. I think a lot more of it now than before I went to Washington. And after a while, when that Exposition is over and the Smithsonian people get home, they would come out here all right. I've learned enough from them so that I could go on with it myself."

Blake reminded me that I had my way to make in the world, and that I wanted to go to school. "That money's in the bank this minute, in your name, and you're going to college on it. You're not going to be a day-labourer like me. After you've got your sheepskin, then you can divide with me."

"You think I'd touch that money?" I looked

squarely at him for the first time. "No more than if you'd stolen it. You made the sale. Get what you can out of it. I want to ask you one question: did you ever think I was digging those things up for what I could sell them for?"

Rodney explained that he knew I cared about the things, and was proud of them, but he'd always supposed I meant to "realize" on them, just as he did, and that it would come to money in the end. "Everything does," he added.

"If that nice young Frenchman I met had come down here with me, and offered me four million instead of four thousand, I'd have refused him. There never was any question of money with me, where this mesa and its people were concerned. They were something that had been preserved through the ages by a miracle, and handed on to you and me, two poor cow-punchers, rough and ignorant, but I thought we were men enough to keep a trust. I'd as soon have sold my own grandmother as Mother Eve—I'd have sold any living woman first."

"Save your tears," said Roddy grimly. "She refused to leave us. She went to the bottom of Black Canyon and carried Hook's best mule along with her. They had to make her box extra wide, and she crowded Jenny out an inch or so too far from the canyon wall."

This painful interview went on for hours. I walked up and down the kitchen trying to make Blake understand the kind of value those objects had had for me. Unfortunately, I succeeded. He sat slumping on the bench, his elbows on the table, shading his eyes from the lantern with his hands.

"There's no need to keep this up," he said at last. "You're away out of my depth, but I think I get you. You might have given me some of this Fourth of July talk a little earlier in the game. I didn't know you valued that stuff any different than anything else a fellow might run on to: a gold mine or a pocket of turquoise."

"I suppose you gave him my diary along with the rest?"

"No," said Blake, his voice growing gloomier and darker, "that's in the Eagle's Nest, where you hid it. That's your private property. I supposed I had some share in the relics we dug up—you always spoke of it that way. But I see now I was working for you like a hired man, and while you were away I sold your property."

I said again it wasn't mine or his. He took something out of the pocket of his flannel shirt and laid it on the table. I saw it was a bank passbook, with my name on the yellow cover.

"You may as well keep it," I said. "I'll never touch it. You had no right to deposit it in my name. The townspeople are sore about the money, and they'll hold it against me."

"No they won't. Can't you trust me to fix that?"

"I don't know what I can trust you with, Blake. I don't know where I'm at with you," I said.

He got up and began putting on his coat. "Motives don't count, eh?" he said, his face turned away, as he put his arm into the sleeve.

"They would in anything of our own, between you and me," I told him. "If it was my money you'd lost gambling, or my girl you'd made free with, we could fight it out, and maybe be friends again. But this is different."

"I see. You make it clear." He was quietly stirring around as he spoke. He got his old knapsack off its nail on the wall, opened his trunk and took out some underwear and socks and a couple of shirts. After he had put these into the bag, he slung it over one shoulder, and his canvas water-bag over the other.

65

I let these preparations go on without a word. He went to the cupboard over the stove and put some sticks of chocolate into his pocket, then his pipe and a bag of tobacco. Presently I said he'd break his neck if he tried riding down the trail in the dark.

"I'm not riding the trail," he replied curtly. "I'm going down the quick way. My horse is grazing in Cow Canyon."

"I noticed the river's high. It's dangerous crossing," I remarked.

"I got over that way a few days ago. I'm surprised at you, using such common expressions!" he said sarcastically. "*Dangerous crossing;* it's painted on signboards all over the world!" He walked out of the cabin without looking back. I followed him to the V-shaped break in the rim rock, hardly larger than a man's body, where the spliced tree-trunks made a swinging ladder down the face of the cliff. I wanted to protest, but only succeeded in finding fault.

"You'll catch your knapsack on those forks and come to grief."

"That's my look-out."

By this time my eyes had grown accustomed to the darkness, and I could see Blake quite clearly—the stubborn, crouching set of his shoulders that I used to notice when he first came to Pardee and was drinking all the time. There was an ache in my arms to reach out and detain him, but there was something else that made me absolutely powerless to do so. He stepped down and settled his foot into the first fork. Then he stopped a moment and straightened his pack, buttoned his coat up to the chin, and pulled his hat on tighter. There was always a night draught in the canyon. He gripped the trunk with his hands. "Well," he said with grim cheerfulness, "here's luck! And I'm glad it's you that's doing this to me, Tom; not me that's doing it to you."

His head disappeared below the rim. I could hear the trees creak under his heavy body, and the chains rattle a little at the splicings. I lay down on the ledge and listened. I could hear him for a long way down, and the sounds were comforting to me, though I didn't realize it. Then the silence closed in. I went to sleep that night hoping I would never waken.

SEVEN/ The next morning the whinnying of my saddle-horse in the shed roused me. I took him down to the foot of the trail where I'd left my trunk, and packed my things up to the cabin on his back. I sat up late that night, waiting for Blake, though I knew he wouldn't come. A few days later I rode into Tarpin for news of him. Bill Hook showed me Roddy's horse. He had sold him to the barn for sixty dollars. The station-master told me Blake had bought a ticket to Winslow, Arizona. I wired the station-master and the dispatcher at Winslow, but they could give me no information. Father Duchene came along, on his rounds, and I told him the whole story.

He thought Blake would come back sometime, that I'd only miss him if I went out to look for him. He advised me to stay on the mesa that summer and get ahead with my studies, work up my Spanish grammar and my Latin. He had friends all along the Santa Fé, and he was sure we could catch Blake by advertising in the local papers along the road; Albuquerque, Winslow, Flagstaff, Williams, Los Angeles. After a few days with him, I went back to the mesa to wait.

I'll never forget the night I got back. I crossed the river an hour before sunset and hobbled my horse in the wide bottom of Cow Canyon. The moon was up, though the sun hadn't set, and it had that glittering silveriness the early stars have in high altitudes. The heavenly bodies look so much more remote from the bottom of a deep canyon than they do from the level. The climb of the walls helps out the eye, somehow. I lay down on a solitary rock that was like an island in the bottom of the valley, and looked up. The grey sage-brush and the blue-grey rock around me were already in shadow, but high above me the canyon walls were dyed flame-colour with the sunset, and the Cliff City lay in a gold haze against its dark cavern. In a few minutes it, too, was grey, and only the rim rock at the top held the red light. When that was gone, I could still see the copper glow in the piñons along the edge of the top ledges. The arc of sky over the canyon was silvery blue, with its pale yellow moon, and presently stars shivered into it, like crystals dropped into perfectly clear water.

I remember these things, because, in a sense, that was the first night I was ever really on the mesa at all—the first night that all of me was there. This was the first time I ever saw it as a whole. It all came together in my understanding, as a series of experiments do when you begin to see where they are leading. Something had happened in me that made it possible for me to co-ordinate and simplify, and that process, going on in my mind, brought with it great happiness. It was possession. The excitement of my first discovery was a very pale feeling compared to this one. For me the mesa was no longer an adventure, but a religious emotion. I had read of filial piety in the Latin poets, and I knew that was what I felt for this place. It had formerly been mixed up with other motives; but now that they were gone, I had my happiness unalloyed.

What that night began lasted all summer. I stayed on the mesa until November. It was the first time I'd ever studied methodically, or intelligently. I got the better of the Spanish grammar and read the twelve books of the *Æneid*. I studied in the morning, and in the afternoon I worked at clearing away the mess the German had made in packing—tidying up the ruins to wait another hundred years, maybe, for the right explorer. I can scarcely hope that life will give me another summer like that one. It was my high tide. Every morning, when the sun's rays first hit the mesa top, while the rest of the world was in shadow, I wakened with the feeling that I had found everything, instead of having lost everything. Nothing tired me. Up there alone, a close neighbour to the sun, I seemed to get the solar energy in some direct way. And at night, when I watched it drop down behind the edge of the plain below me, I used to feel that I couldn't have borne another hour of that consuming light, that I was full to the brim, and needed dark and sleep.

All that summer, I never went up to the Eagle's Nest to get my diary—indeed, it's probably there yet. I didn't feel the need of that record. It would have been going backward. I didn't want to go back and unravel things step by step. Perhaps I was afraid that I would lose the whole in the parts. At any rate, I didn't go for my record.

During those months I didn't worry much about poor Roddy. I told myself the advertisements would surely get him—I knew his habit of reading newspapers. There are times when one's vitality is too high to be clouded, too elastic to stay down. Hurrying from my cabin in the morning to the spot in the Cliff City where I studied under a cedar, I used to be frightened at my own heartlessness. But the feel of the narrow moccasin-worn trail in the flat rock made my feet glad, like a good taste in the mouth, and I'd forget all about Blake without knowing it. I found I was reading too fast; so I began to commit long passages of Virgil to memory—if it hadn't been for that, I might have forgotten how to use my voice, or gone to talking to myself. When I look into the *Æneid* now, I can always see two pictures: the one on the page, and another behind that: blue and purple rocks and yellow-green piñons with flat tops, little clustered houses clinging together for protection, a rude tower rising in their midst, rising strong, with calmness and courage—behind it a dark grotto, in its depths a crystal spring.

Happiness is something one can't explain. You must take my word for it. Troubles enough came afterward, but there was that summer, high and blue, a life in itself.

Next winter I went back to Pardee and stayed with the O'Briens again, working on the section and studying with Father Duchene and trying to get some word of Blake. Now that I was back on the railroad, I thought I couldn't fail to find him. I went out to Winslow and to Williams, and I questioned the railroad men. We advertised for him in every possible way, had all the Santa Fé operatives and the police and the Catholic missionaries on the watch for him, offered a thousand dollars reward for whoever found him. But it came to nothing. Father Duchene and our friends down there are still looking. But the older I grow, the more I understand what it was I did that night on the mesa. Anyone who requites faith and friendship as I did, will have to pay for it. I'm not very sanguine about good fortune for myself. I'll be called to account when I least expect it.

In the spring, just a year after I quarrelled with Roddy, I landed here and walked into your garden, and the rest you know.

*Neighbour Rosicky**

O N E /   When Doctor Burleigh told neighbour Rosicky he had a bad heart, Rosicky protested.

"So? No, I guess my heart was always pretty good. I got a little asthma, maybe. Just a awful short breath when I was pitchin' hay last summer, dat's all."

"Well now, Rosicky, if you know more about it than I do, what did you come to me for? It's your heart that makes you short of breath, I tell you. You're sixty-five years old, and you've always worked hard, and your heart's tired. You've got to be careful from now on, and you can't do heavy work any more. You've got five boys at home to do it for you."

The old farmer looked up at the Doctor with a gleam of amusement in his queer triangular-shaped eyes. His eyes were large and lively, but the lids were caught up in the middle in a curious way, so that they formed a triangle. He did not look like a sick man. His brown face was creased but not wrinkled, he had a ruddy colour in his smooth-

*From *Obscure Destinies*, 1932.

shaven cheeks and in his lips, under his long brown moustache. His hair was thin and ragged around his ears, but very little grey. His forehead, naturally high and crossed by deep parallel lines, now ran all the way up to his pointed crown. Rosicky's face had the habit of looking interested,—suggested a contented disposition and a reflective quality that was gay rather than grave. This gave him a certain detachment, the easy manner of an onlooker and observer.

"Well, I guess you ain't got no pills fur a bad heart, Doctor Ed. I guess the only thing is fur me to git me a new one."

Doctor Burleigh swung round in his desk-chair and frowned at the old farmer. "I think if I were you I'd take a little care of the old one, Rosicky."

Rosicky shrugged. "Maybe I don't know how. I expect you mean fur me not to drink my coffee no more."

"I wouldn't, in your place. But you'll do as you choose about that. I've never yet been able to separate a Bohemian from his coffee or his pipe. I've quit trying. But the sure thing is you've got to cut out farm work. You can feed the stock and do chores about the barn, but you can't do anything in the fields that makes you short of breath."

"How about shelling corn?"

"Of course not!"

Rosicky considered with puckered brows.

"I can't make my heart go no longer'n it wants to, can I, Doctor Ed?"

"I think it's good for five or six years yet, maybe more, if you'll take the strain off it. Sit around the house and help Mary. If I had a good wife like yours, I'd want to stay around the house."

His patient chuckled. "It ain't no place fur a man. I don't like no old man hanging round the kitchen

73

too much. An' my wife, she's a awful hard worker her own self."

"That's it; you can help her a little. My Lord, Rosicky, you are one of the few men I know who has a family he can get some comfort out of; happy dispositions, never quarrel among themselves, and they treat you right. I want to see you live a few years and enjoy them."

"Oh, they're good kids, all right," Rosicky assented.

The Doctor wrote him a prescription and asked him how his oldest son, Rudolph, who had married in the spring, was getting on. Rudolph had struck out for himself, on rented land. "And how's Polly? I was afraid Mary mightn't like an American daughter-in-law, but it seems to be working out all right."

"Yes, she's a fine girl. Dat widder woman bring her daughters up very nice. Polly got lots of spunk, an' she got some style, too. Da's nice, for young folks to have some style." Rosicky inclined his head gallantly. His voice and his twinkly smile were an affectionate compliment to his daughter-in-law.

"It looks like a storm, and you'd better be getting home before it comes. In town in the car?" Doctor Burleigh rose.

"No, I'm in de wagon. When you got five boys, you ain't got much chance to ride round in de Ford. I ain't much for cars, noway."

"Well, it's a good road out to your place; but I don't want you bumping around in a wagon much. And never again on a hay-rake, remember!"

Rosicky placed the Doctor's fee delicately behind the desk-telephone, looking the other way, as if this were an absent-minded gesture. He put on his plush cap and his corduroy jacket with a sheepskin collar, and went out.

The Doctor picked up his stethoscope and frowned at it as if he were seriously annoyed with the instrument. He wished it had been telling tales about some other man's heart, some old man who didn't look the Doctor in the eye so knowingly, or hold out such a warm brown hand when he said good-bye. Doctor Burleigh had been a poor boy in the country before he went away to medical school; he had known Rosicky almost ever since he could remember, and he had a deep affection for Mrs. Rosicky.

Only last winter he had had such a good breakfast at Rosicky's, and that when he needed it. He had been out all night on a long, hard confinement case at Tom Marshall's,—a big rich farm where there was plenty of stock and plenty of feed and a great deal of expensive farm machinery of the newest model, and no comfort whatever. The woman had too many children and too much work, and she was no manager. When the baby was born at last, and handed over to the assisting neighbour woman, and the mother was properly attended to, Burleigh refused any breakfast in that slovenly house, and drove his buggy—the snow was too deep for a car—eight miles to Anton Rosicky's place. He didn't know another farm-house where a man could get such a warm welcome, and such good strong coffee with rich cream. No wonder the old chap didn't want to give up his coffee!

He had driven in just when the boys had come back from the barn and were washing up for breakfast. The long table, covered with a bright oilcloth, was set out with dishes waiting for them, and the warm kitchen was full of the smell of coffee and hot biscuit and sausage. Five big handsome boys, running from twenty to twelve, all with what Burleigh called natural good manners,—they hadn't a bit of the painful self-consciousness he himself had to struggle with when he was a lad. One ran to put his horse away, another helped him off with his fur coat and hung it up, and Josephine, the youngest child and the only daughter, quickly set another place under her mother's direction.

With Mary, to feed creatures was the natural expression of affection,—her chickens, the calves, her big hungry boys. It was a rare pleasure to feed a young man whom she seldom saw and of whom she was as proud as if he belonged to her. Some country housekeepers would have stopped to spread a white cloth over the oilcloth, to change the thick cups and plates for their best china, and the wooden-handled knives for plated ones. But not Mary.

"You must take us as you find us, Doctor Ed. I'd be glad to put out my good things for you if you was expected, but I'm glad to get you any way at all."

He knew she was glad,—she threw back her head and spoke out as if she were announcing him to the whole prairie. Rosicky hadn't said anything at all; he merely smiled his twinkling smile, put some more coal on the fire, and went into his own room to pour the Doctor a little drink in a medicine glass. When they were all seated, he watched his wife's face from his end of the table and spoke to her in Czech. Then, with the instinct of politeness which seldom failed him, he turned to the Doctor and said slyly: "I was just tellin' her not to ask you no questions about Mrs. Marshall till you eat some breakfast. My wife, she's terrible fur to ask questions."

The boys laughed, and so did Mary. She watched the Doctor devour her biscuit and sausage, too much excited to eat anything herself. She drank her coffee and sat taking in everything about her visitor. She had known him when he was a poor country boy, and was boastfully proud of his success, always saying: "What do people go to Omaha for, to see a doctor, when we got the best one in the State right here?" If Mary liked people at all, she felt physical pleasure in the sight of them, personal exultation in any good fortune that came to them. Burleigh didn't know many women like that, but he knew she was like that.

When his hunger was satisfied, he did, of course, have to tell them about Mrs. Marshall, and he noticed what a friendly interest the boys took in the matter.

Rudolph, the oldest one (he was still living at home then), said: "The last time I was over there, she was lifting them big heavy milk-cans, and I knew she oughtn't to be doing it."

"Yes, Rudolph told me about that when he came home, and I said it wasn't right," Mary put in warmly. "It was all right for me to do them things up to the last, for I was terrible strong, but that woman's weakly. And do you think she'll be able to nurse it, Ed?" She sometimes forgot to give him the title she was so proud of. "And to think of your being up all night and then not able to get a decent breakfast! I don't know what's the matter with such people."

"Why, Mother," said one of the boys, "if Doctor Ed had got breakfast there, we wouldn't have him here. So you ought to be glad."

"He knows I'm glad to have him, John, any time. But I'm sorry for that poor woman, how bad she'll feel the Doctor had to go away in the cold without his breakfast."

"I wish I'd been in practice when these were getting born." The doctor looked down the row of close-clipped heads. "I missed some good breakfasts by not being."

The boys began to laugh at their mother because she flushed so red, but she stood her ground and threw up her head. "I don't care, you wouldn't have got away from this house without breakfast. No doctor ever did. I'd have had something ready fixed that Anton could warm up for you."

The boys laughed harder than ever, and exclaimed

at her: "I'll bet you would!" "She would, that!"

"Father, did you get breakfast for the doctor when we were born?"

"Yes, and he used to bring me my breakfast, too, mighty nice. I was always awful hungry!" Mary admitted with a guilty laugh.

While the boys were getting the Doctor's horse, he went to the window to examine the house plants. "What do you do to your geraniums to keep them blooming all winter, Mary? I never pass this house that from the road I don't see your windows full of flowers."

She snapped off a dark red one, and a ruffled new green leaf, and put them in his buttonhole. "There, that looks better. You look too solemn for a young man, Ed. Why don't you git married? I'm worried about you. Settin' at breakfast, I looked at you real hard, and I seen you've got some grey hairs already."

"Oh, yes! They're coming. Maybe they'd come faster if I married."

"Don't talk so. You'll ruin your health eating at the hotel. I could send your wife a nice loaf of nut bread, if you only had one. I don't like to see a young man getting grey. I'll tell you something, Ed; you make some strong black tea and keep it handy in a bowl, and every morning just brush it into your hair, an' it'll keep the grey from showin' much. That's the way I do!"

Sometimes the Doctor heard tne gossipers in the drug-store wondering why Rosicky didn't get on faster. He was industrious, and so were his boys, but they were rather free and easy, weren't pushers, and they didn't always show good judgment. They were comfortable, they were out of debt, but they didn't get much ahead. Maybe, Doctor Burleigh reflected, people as generous and warm-hearted and affectionate as the Rosickys never got ahead much; maybe you couldn't enjoy your life and put it into the bank, too.

TWO / When Rosicky left Doctor Burleigh's office he went into the farm-implement store to light his pipe and put on his glasses and read over the list Mary had given him. Then he went into the general merchandise place next door and stood about until the pretty girl with the plucked eyebrows, who always waited on him, was free. Those eyebrows, two thin India-ink strokes, amused him, because he remembered how they used to be. Rosicky always prolonged his shopping by a little joking; the girl knew the old fellow admired her, and she liked to chaff with him.

"Seems to me about every other week you buy ticking, Mr. Rosicky, and always the best quality," she remarked as she measured off the heavy bolt with red stripes.

"You see, my wife is always makin' goose-fedder pillows, an' de thin stuff don't hold in dem little down-fedders."

"You must have lots of pillows at your house."

"Sure. She makes quilts of dem, too. We sleeps easy. Now she's makin' a fedder quilt for my son's wife. You know Polly, that married my Rudolph. How much my bill, Miss Pearl?"

"Eight eighty-five."

"Chust make it nine, and put in some candy fur de women."

"As usual. I never did see a man buy so much

candy for his wife. First thing you know, she'll be getting too fat."

"I'd like dat. I ain't much fur all dem slim women like what de style is now."

"That's one for me, I suppose, Mr. Bohunk!" Pearl sniffed and elevated her India-ink strokes.

When Rosicky went out to his wagon, it was beginning to snow,—the first snow of the season, and he was glad to see it. He rattled out of town and along the highway through a wonderfully rich stretch of country, the finest farms in the county. He admired this High Prairie, as it was called, and always liked to drive through it. His own place lay in a rougher territory, where there was some clay in the soil and it was not so productive. When he bought his land, he hadn't the money to buy on High Prairie; so he told his boys, when they grumbled, that if their land hadn't some clay in it, they wouldn't own it at all. All the same, he enjoyed looking at these fine farms, as he enjoyed looking at a prize bull.

After he had gone eight miles, he came to the graveyard, which lay just at the edge of his own hay-land. There he stopped his horses and sat still on his wagon seat, looking about at the snowfall. Over yonder on the hill he could see his own house, crouching low, with the clump of orchard behind and the windmill before, and all down the gentle hill-slope the rows of pale gold cornstalks stood out against the white field. The snow was falling over the cornfield and the pasture and the hay-land, steadily, with very little wind,—a nice dry snow. The graveyard had only a light wire fence about it and was all overgrown with long red grass. The fine snow, settling into this red grass and upon the few little evergreens and the headstones, looked very pretty.

It was a nice graveyard, Rosicky reflected, sort of
snug and homelike, not cramped or mournful,—a big
sweep all round it. A man could lie down in the long
grass and see the complete arch of the sky over him,
hear the wagons go by; in summer the mowing-
machine rattled right up to the wire fence. And it
was so near home. Over there across the cornstalks
his own roof and windmill looked so good to him
that he promised himself to mind the Doctor and
take care of himself. He was awful fond of his place,
he admitted. He wasn't anxious to leave it. And it
was a comfort to think that he would never have to
go farther than the edge of his own hayfield. The
snow, falling over his barnyard and the graveyard,
seemed to draw things together like. And they were
all old neighbours in the graveyard, most of them
friends; there was nothing to feel awkward or embarrassed about. Embarrassment was the most dis-
agreeable feeling Rosicky knew. He didn't often have
it,—only with certain people whom he didn't understand at all.

Well, it was a nice snowstorm; a fine sight to see
the snow falling so quietly and graciously over so
much open country. On his cap and shoulders, on the
horses' backs and manes, light, delicate, mysterious
it fell; and with it a dry cool fragrance was released
into the air. It meant rest for vegetation and men and
beasts, for the ground itself; a season of long nights
for sleep, leisurely breakfasts, peace by the fire. This
and much more went through Rosicky's mind, but
he merely told himself that winter was coming,
clucked to his horses, and drove on.

When he reached home, John, the youngest boy,
ran out to put away his team for him, and he met
Mary coming up from the outside cellar with her
apron full of carrots. They went into the house

together. On the table, covered with oilcloth figured with clusters of blue grapes, a place was set, and he smelled hot coffee-cake of some kind. Anton never lunched in town; he thought that extravagant, and anyhow he didn't like the food. So Mary always had something ready for him when he got home.

After he was settled in his chair, stirring his coffee in a big cup, Mary took out of the oven a pan of *kolache* stuffed with apricots, examined them anxiously to see whether they had got too dry, put them beside his plate, and then sat down opposite him.

Rosicky asked her in Czech if she wasn't going to have any coffee.

She replied in English, as being somehow the right language for transacting business: "Now what did Doctor Ed say, Anton? You tell me just what."

"He said I was to tell you some compliments, but I forgot 'em." Rosicky's eyes twinkled.

"About you, I mean. What did he say about your asthma?"

"He says I ain't got no asthma." Rosicky took one of the little rolls in his broad brown fingers. The thickened nail of his right thumb told the story of his past.

"Well, what is the matter? And don't try to put me off."

"He don't say nothing much, only I'm a little older, and my heart ain't so good like it used to be."

Mary started and brushed her hair back from her temples with both hands as if she were a little out of her mind. From the way she glared, she might have been in a rage with him.

"He says there's something the matter with your heart? Doctor Ed says so?"

"Now don't yell at me like I was a hog in de garden, Mary. You know I always did like to hear a woman talk soft. He didn't say anything de matter wid my heart, only it ain't so young like it used to be, an' he tell me not to pitch hay or run de corn-sheller."

Mary wanted to jump up, but she sat still. She admired the way he never under any circumstances raised his voice or spoke roughly. He was city-bred, and she was country-bred; she often said she wanted her boys to have their papa's nice ways.

"You never have no pain there, do you? It's your breathing and your stomach that's been wrong. I wouldn't believe nobody but Doctor Ed about it. I guess I'll go see him myself. Didn't he give you no advice?"

"Chust to take it easy like, an' stay round de house dis winter. I guess you got some carpenter work for me to do. I kin make some new shelves for you, and I want dis long time to build a closet in de boys' room and make dem two little fellers keep dere clo'es hung up."

Rosicky drank his coffee from time to time, while he considered. His moustache was of the soft long variety and came down over his mouth like the teeth of a buggy-rake over a bundle of hay. Each time he put down his cup, he ran his blue handkerchief over his lips. When he took a drink of water, he managed very neatly with the back of his hand.

Mary sat watching him intently, trying to find any change in his face. It is hard to see anyone who has become like your own body to you. Yes, his hair had got thin, and his high forehead had deep lines running from left to right. But his neck, always clean shaved except in the busiest seasons, was not loose or baggy. It was burned a dark reddish brown, and there were deep creases in it, but it looked firm and full of blood. His cheeks had a good colour. On either side of his mouth there was a half-moon down the length of his cheek, not wrinkles, but two lines that had come there from his habitual expression. He was shorter and broader than when she married him; his back had grown broad and curved, a good deal like the shell of an old turtle, and his arms and legs were short.

He was fifteen years older than Mary, but she had hardly ever thought about it before. He was her man, and the kind of man she liked. She was rough, and he was gentle,—city-bred, as she always said. They had been shipmates on a rough voyage and had stood by each other in trying times. Life had gone well with them because, at bottom, they had the same ideas about life. They agreed, without discussion, as to what was most important and what was secondary. They didn't often exchange opinions, even in Czech,—it was as if they had thought the same thought together. A good deal had to be sacrificed and thrown overboard in a hard life like theirs, and they had never disagreed as to the things that could go. It had been a hard life, and a soft life, too. There wasn't anything brutal in the short, broad-backed man with the three-cornered eyes and the forehead that went on to the top of his skull. He was a city man, a gentle man, and though he had married a rough farm girl, he had never touched her without gentleness.

They had been at one accord not to hurry through life, not to be always skimping and saving. They saw their neighbours buy more land and feed more stock than they did, without discontent. Once when the creamery agent came to the Rosickys to persuade them to sell him their cream, he told them how much money the Fasslers, their nearest neighbours, had made on their cream last year.

"Yes," said Mary, "and look at them Fassler children! Pale, pinched little things, they look like skimmed milk. I'd rather put some colour into my children's faces than put money into the bank."

The agent shrugged and turned to Anton.

"I guess we'll do like she says," said Rosicky.

THREE / Mary very soon got into town to
see Doctor Ed, and then she had a talk with her boys
and set a guard over Rosicky. Even John, the youngest, had his father on his mind. If Rosicky went to
throw hay down from the loft, one of the boys ran
up the ladder and took the fork from him. He sometimes complained that though he was getting to be an
old man, he wasn't an old woman yet.

That winter he stayed in the house in the afternoons
and carpentered, or sat in the chair between the window full of plants and the wooden bench where the
two pails of drinking water stood. This spot was called
"Father's corner," though it was not a corner at all.
He had a shelf there, where he kept his Bohemian
papers and his pipes and tobacco, and his shears and
needles and thread and tailor's thimble. Having been a
tailor in his youth, he couldn't bear to see a woman
patching at his clothes, or at the boys'. He liked tailoring, and always patched all the overalls and jackets and
work shirts. Occasionally he made over a pair of pants
one of the older boys had outgrown, for the little
fellow.

While he sewed, he let his mind run back over his
life. He had a good deal to remember, really; life in
three countries. The only part of his youth he didn't
like to remember was the two years he had spent in
London, in Cheapside, working for a German tailor
who was wretchedly poor. Those days, when he was
nearly always hungry, when his clothes were dropping off him for dirt, and the sound of a strange language kept him in continual bewilderment, had left
a sore spot in his mind that wouldn't bear touching.

He was twenty when he landed at Castle Garden
in New York, and he had a protector who got him

work in a tailor shop in Vesey Street, down near the Washington Market. He looked upon that part of his life as very happy. He became a good workman, he was industrious, and his wages were increased from time to time. He minded his own business and envied nobody's good fortune. He went to night school and learned to read English. He often did overtime work and was well paid for it, but somehow he never saved anything. He couldn't refuse a loan to a friend, and he was self-indulgent. He liked a good dinner, and a little went for beer, a little for tobacco; a good deal went to the girls. He often stood through an opera on Saturday nights; he could get standing-room for a dollar. Those were the great days of opera in New York, and it gave a fellow something to think about for the rest of the week. Rosicky had a quick ear, and a childish love of all the stage splendour; the scenery, the costumes, the ballet. He usually went with a chum, and after the performance they had beer and maybe some oysters somewhere. It was a fine life; for the first five years or so it satisfied him completely. He was never hungry or cold or dirty, and everything amused him: a fire, a dog fight, a parade, a storm, a ferry ride. He thought New York the finest, richest, friendliest city in the world.

Moreover, he had what he called a happy home life. Very near the tailor shop was a small furniture-factory, where an old Austrian, Loeffler, employed a few skilled men and made unusual furniture, most of it to order, for the rich German housewives up-town. The top floor of Loeffler's five-storey factory was a loft, where he kept his choice lumber and stored the odd pieces of furniture left on his hands. One of the young workmen he employed was a Czech, and he and Rosicky became fast friends. They persuaded Loeffler to let them have a sleeping-room in one corner of the loft. They bought good beds and bedding and had their pick of the furniture kept up there. The loft was low-pitched, but light and airy, full of windows, and good-smelling by reason of the fine lumber put up there to season. Old Loeffler used to go down to the docks and buy wood from South America and the East from the sea captains. The young men were as foolish about their house as a bridal pair. Zichec, the young cabinet-maker, devised every sort of convenience, and Rosicky kept their clothes in order. At night and on Sundays, when the quiver of machinery underneath was still, it was the quietest place in the world, and on summer nights all the sea winds blew in. Zichec often practised on his flute in the evening. They were both fond of music and went to the opera together. Rosicky thought he wanted to live like that for ever.

But as the years passed, all alike, he began to get a little restless. When spring came round, he would begin to feel fretted, and he got to drinking. He was likely to drink too much of a Saturday night. On Sunday he was languid and heavy, getting over his spree. On Monday he plunged into work again. So he never had time to figure out what ailed him, though he knew something did. When the grass turned green in Park Place, and the lilac hedge at the back of Trinity churchyard put out its blossoms, he was tormented by a longing to run away. That was why he drank too much; to get a temporary illusion of freedom and wide horizons.

Rosicky, the old Rosicky, could remember as if it were yesterday the day when the young Rosicky found out what was the matter with him. It was on a Fourth of July afternoon, and he was sitting in Park Place in the sun. The lower part of New York was empty. Wall Street, Liberty Street, Broadway, all empty. So much stone and asphalt with nothing going on, so many empty windows. The emptiness was intense, like the stillness in a great factory when the machinery stops and the belts and bands cease running. It was too great a change, it took all the strength out of one. Those blank buildings, without the stream of life pouring through them, were like empty jails. It struck young Rosicky that this was the trouble with big cities; they built you in from the earth itself, cemented you away from any contact with the ground. You lived in an unnatural world, like the fish in an aquarium, who were probably much more comfortable than they ever were in the sea.

On that very day he began to think seriously about the articles he had read in the Bohemian papers, describing prosperous Czech farming communities in the West. He believed he would like to go out there as a farm hand; it was hardly possible that he could ever have land of his own. His people had always been workmen; his father and grandfather had worked in shops. His mother's parents had lived in the country, but they rented their farm and had a hard time to get along. Nobody in his family had ever owned any land, —that belonged to a different station of life altogether. Anton's mother died when he was little, and he was sent into the country to her parents. He stayed with them until he was twelve, and formed those ties with the earth and the farm animals and growing things which are never made at all unless they are made early. After his grandfather died, he went back to live with his father and stepmother, but she was very hard on him, and his father helped him to get passage to London.

After that Fourth of July day in Park Place, the desire to return to the country never left him. To work on another man's farm would be all he asked; to see the sun rise and set and to plant things and watch them grow. He was a very simple man. He was like a tree that has not many roots, but one tap-root that goes down deep. He subscribed for a Bohemian paper printed in Chicago, then for one printed in Omaha. His mind got farther and farther west. He began to save a little money to buy his liberty. When he was thirty-five, there was a great meeting in New York of Bohemian athletic societies, and Rosicky left the tailor shop and went home with the Omaha delegates to try his fortune in another part of the world.

FOUR/ Perhaps the fact that his own youth was well over before he began to have a family was one reason why Rosicky was so fond of his boys. He had almost a grandfather's indulgence for them. He had never had to worry about any of them—except, just now, a little about Rudolph.

On Saturday night the boys always piled into the Ford, took little Josephine, and went to town to the moving-picture show. One Saturday morning they were talking at the breakfast table about starting early that evening, so that they would have an hour or so to see the Christmas things in the stores before the show began. Rosicky looked down the table.

"I hope you boys ain't disappointed, but I want you to let me have de car tonight. Maybe some of you can go in with de neighbours."

Their faces fell. They worked hard all week, and they were still like children. A new jackknife or a box of candy pleased the older ones as much as the little fellow.

"If you and Mother are going to town," Frank said, "maybe you could take a couple of us along with you, anyway."

"No, I want to take de car down to Rudolph's, and

let him an' Polly go in to de show. She don't git into town enough, an' I'm afraid she's gettin' lonesome, an' he can't afford no car yet."

That settled it. The boys were a good deal dashed. Their father took another piece of apple-cake and went on: "Maybe next Saturday night de two little fellers can go along wid dem."

"Oh, is Rudolph going to have the car every Saturday night?"

Rosicky did not reply at once; then he began to speak seriously: "Listen, boys; Polly ain't lookin' so good. I don't like to see nobody lookin' sad. It comes hard fur a town girl to be a farmer's wife. I don't want no trouble to start in Rudolph's family. When it starts, it ain't so easy to stop. An American girl don't git used to our ways all at once. I like to tell Polly she and Rudolph can have the car every Saturday night till after New Year's, if it's all right with you boys."

"Sure it's all right, Papa," Mary cut in. "And it's good you thought about that. Town girls is used to more than country girls. I lay awake nights, scared she'll make Rudolph discontented with the farm."

The boys put as good a face on it as they could. They surely looked forward to their Saturday nights in town. That evening Rosicky drove the car the half-mile down to Rudolph's new, bare little house.

Polly was in a short-sleeved gingham dress, clearing away the supper dishes. She was a trim, slim little thing, with blue eyes and shingled yellow hair, and her eyebrows were reduced to a mere brush-stroke, like Miss Pearl's.

"Good evening, Mr. Rosicky. Rudolph's at the barn, I guess." She never called him father, or Mary mother. She was sensitive about having married a foreigner. She never in the world would have done it if Rudolph hadn't been such a handsome, persuasive fellow and such a gallant lover. He had graduated in her class in the high school in town, and their friendship began in the ninth grade.

Rosicky went in, though he wasn't exactly asked. "My boys ain't goin' to town tonight, an' I brought de car over fur you two to go in to de picture show."

Polly, carrying dishes to the sink, looked over her shoulder at him. "Thank you. But I'm late with my work tonight, and pretty tired. Maybe Rudolph would like to go in with you."

"Oh, I don't go to de shows! I'm too old-fashioned. You won't feel so tired after you ride in de air a ways. It's a nice clear night, an' it ain't cold. You go an' fix yourself up, Polly, an' I'll wash de dishes an' leave everything nice fur you."

Polly blushed and tossed her bob. "I couldn't let you do that, Mr. Rosicky. I wouldn't think of it."

Rosicky said nothing. He found a bib apron on a nail behind the kitchen door. He slipped it over his head and then took Polly by her two elbows and pushed her gently toward the door of her own room. "I washed up de kitchen many times for my wife, when de babies was sick or somethin'. You go an' make yourself look nice. I like you to look prettier'n any of dem town girls when you go in. De young folks must have some fun, an' I'm goin' to look out fur you, Polly."

That kind, reassuring grip on her elbows, the old man's funny bright eyes, made Polly want to drop her head on his shoulder for a second. She restrained herself, but she lingered in his grasp at the door of her room, murmuring tearfully: "You always lived in the city when you were young, didn't you? Don't you ever get lonesome out here?"

As she turned round to him, her hand fell naturally into his, and he stood holding it and smiling into her face with his peculiar, knowing, indulgent smile without a shadow of reproach in it. "Dem big cities is all right fur de rich, but dey is terrible hard fur de poor."

"I don't know. Sometimes I think I'd like to take a chance. You lived in New York, didn't you?"

"An' London. Da's bigger still. I learned my trade dere. Here's Rudolph comin', you better hurry."

"Will you tell me about London some time?"

"Maybe. Only I ain't no talker, Polly. Run an' dress yourself up."

The bedroom door closed behind her, and Rudolph came in from the outside, looking anxious. He had seen the car and was sorry any of his family should come just then. Supper hadn't been a very pleasant occasion. Halting in the doorway, he saw his father in a kitchen apron, carrying dishes to the sink. He flushed crimson and something flashed in his eye. Rosicky held up a warning finger.

"I brought de car over fur you an' Polly to go to de picture show, an' I made her let me finish here so you won't be late. You go put on a clean shirt, quick!"

"But don't the boys want the car, Father?"

"Not tonight dey don't." Rosicky fumbled under his apron and found his pants pocket. He took out a silver dollar and said in a hurried whisper: "You go an' buy dat girl some ice cream an' candy tonight, like you was courtin'. She's awful good friends wid me."

Rudolph was very short of cash, but he took the money as if it hurt him. There had been a crop failure all over the county. He had more than once been sorry he'd married this year.

In a few minutes the young people came out, looking clean and a little stiff. Rosicky hurried them off, and then he took his own time with the dishes. He scoured the pots and pans and put away the milk and swept the kitchen. He put some coal in the stove and shut off the draughts, so the place would be warm for them when they got home late at night. Then he sat down and had a pipe and listened to the clock tick.

Generally speaking, marrying an American girl was certainly a risk. A Czech should marry a Czech. It was lucky that Polly was the daughter of a poor widow woman; Rudolph was proud, and if she had a prosperous family to throw up at him, they could never make it go. Polly was one of four sisters, and they all worked; one was book-keeper in the bank, one taught music, and Polly and her younger sister had been clerks, like Miss Pearl. All four of them were musical, had pretty voices, and sang in the Methodist choir, which the eldest sister directed.

Polly missed the sociability of a store position. She missed the choir, and the company of her sisters. She didn't dislike housework, but she disliked so much of it. Rosicky was a little anxious about this pair. He was afraid Polly would grow so discontented that Rudy would quit the farm and take a factory job in Omaha. He had worked for a winter up there, two years ago, to get money to marry on. He had done very well, and they would always take him back at the stockyards. But to Rosicky that meant the end of everything for his son. To be a landless man was to be a wage-earner, a slave, all your life; to have nothing, to be nothing.

Rosicky thought he would come over and do a little carpentering for Polly after the New Year. He guessed she needed jollying. Rudolph was a serious sort of chap, serious in love and serious about his work.

Rosicky shook out his pipe and walked home across the fields. Ahead of him the lamplight shone from his kitchen windows. Suppose he were still in a tailor shop on Vesey Street, with a bunch of pale, narrow-chested sons working on machines, all coming home tired and sullen to eat supper in a kitchen that was a parlour also; with another crowded, angry family quarrelling just across the dumb-waiter shaft, and squeaking pulleys at the windows where dirty washings hung on dirty lines above a court full of old brooms and mops and ash-cans. . . .

He stopped by the windmill to look up at the frosty winter stars and draw a long breath before he went inside. That kitchen with the shining windows was dear to him; but the sleeping fields and bright stars and the noble darkness were dearer still.

FIVE/   On the day before Christmas the weather set in very cold; no snow, but a bitter, biting wind that whistled and sang over the flat land and lashed one's face like fine wires. There was baking going on in the Rosicky kitchen all day, and Rosicky sat inside, making over a coat that Albert had outgrown into an overcoat for John. Mary had a big red geranium in bloom for Christmas, and a row of Jerusalem cherry trees, full of berries. It was the first year she had ever grown these; Doctor Ed brought her the seeds from Omaha when he went to some medical convention. They reminded Rosicky of plants he had seen in England; and all afternoon, as he stitched, he sat thinking about those two years in London, which his mind usually shrank from even after all this while.

He was a lad of eighteen when he dropped down into London, with no money and no connexions except the address of a cousin who was supposed to be working at a confectioner's. When he went to the pastry shop, however, he found that the cousin had gone to America. Anton tramped the streets for several days, sleeping in doorways and on the Embankment, until he was in utter despair. He knew no English, and the sound of the strange language all about him confused him. By chance he met a poor German tailor who had learned his trade in Vienna, and could speak a little Czech. This tailor, Lifschnitz, kept a repair shop in a Cheapside basement, underneath a cobbler. He didn't much need an apprentice, but he was sorry for the boy and took him in for no wages but his keep and what he could pick up. The pickings were supposed to be coppers given you when you took work home to a customer. But most of the customers called for their clothes themselves, and the coppers that came Anton's way were very few. He had, however, a place to sleep. The tailor's family lived upstairs in three rooms; a kitchen, a bedroom, where Lifschnitz and his wife and five children slept, and a living-room. Two corners of this living-room were curtained off for lodgers; in one Rosicky slept on an old horsehair sofa, with a feather quilt to wrap himself in. The other corner was rented to a wretched, dirty boy, who was studying the violin. He actually·practised there. Rosicky was dirty, too. There was no way to be any-thing else. Mrs. Lifschnitz got the water she cooked and washed with from a pump in a brick court, four flights down. There were bugs in the place, and mul-titudes of fleas, though the poor woman did the best she could. Rosicky knew she often went empty to give another potato or a spoonful of dripping to the two hungry, sad-eyed boys who lodged with her. He used to think he would never get out of there, never get a clean shirt to his back again. What would he do, he wondered, when his clothes actually dropped to pieces and the worn cloth wouldn't hold patches any longer?

It was still early when the old farmer put aside his sewing and his recollections. The sky had been a dark grey all day, with not a gleam of sun, and the light failed at four o'clock. He went to shave and change his shirt while the turkey was roasting. Rudolph and Polly were coming over for supper.

After supper they sat round in the kitchen, and the younger boys were saying how sorry they were it hadn't snowed. Everybody was sorry. They wanted a deep snow that would lie long and keep the wheat warm, and leave the ground soaked when it melted.

"Yes, sir!" Rudolph broke out fiercely; "if we have another dry year like last year, there's going to be hard times in this country."

Rosicky filled his pipe. "You boys don't know what hard times is. You don't owe nobody, you got plenty to eat an' keep warm, an' plenty water to keep clean. When you got them, you can't have it very hard."

Rudolph frowned, opened and shut his big right hand, and dropped it clenched upon his knee. "I've got to have a good deal more than that, Father, or I'll quit this farming gamble. I can always make good wages railroading, or at the packing house, and be sure of my money."

"Maybe so," his father answered dryly.

Mary, who had just come in from the pantry and was wiping her hands on the roller towel, thought Rudy and his father were getting too serious. She brought her darning-basket and sat down in the middle of the group.

"I ain't much afraid of hard times, Rudy," she said heartily. "We've had a plenty, but we've always come through. Your father wouldn't never take nothing very hard, not even hard times. I got a mind to tell you a story on him. Maybe you boys can't hardly remember the year we had that terrible hot wind, that burned everything up on the Fourth of July? All the corn an' the gardens. An' that was in the days when we didn't have alfalfa yet,—I guess it wasn't invented.

"Well, that very day your father was out cultivatin'
corn, and I was here in the kitchen makin' plum pre-
serves. We had bushels of plums that year. I noticed it
was terrible hot, but it's always hot in the kitchen
when you're preservin', an' I was too busy with my
plums to mind. Anton come in from the field about
three o'clock, an' I asked him what was the matter.

" 'Nothin',' he says, 'but it's pretty hot, an' I think
I won't work no more today.' He stood round for
a few minutes, an' then he says: 'Ain't you near
through? I want you should git up a nice supper for
us tonight. It's Fourth of July.'

"I told him to git along, that I was right in the
middle of preservin', but the plums would taste good
on hot biscuit. 'I'm goin' to have fried chicken, too,' he
says, and he went off an' killed a couple. You three
oldest boys was little fellers, playin' round outside,
real hot an' sweaty, an' your father took you to the
horse tank down by the windmill an' took off your
clothes an' put you in. Them two box-elder trees was
little then, but they made shade over the tank. Then
he took off all his own clothes, an' got in with you.
While he was playin' in the water with you, the
Methodist preacher drove into our place to say how
all the neighbours was goin' to meet at the schoolhouse that night, to pray for rain. He drove right to
the windmill, of course, and there was your father
and you three with no clothes on. I was in the kitchen
door, an' I had to laugh, for the preacher acted like
he ain't never seen a naked man before. He surely was
embarrassed, an' your father couldn't git to his clothes;
they was all hangin' up on the windmill to let the
sweat dry out of 'em. So he laid in the tank where he
was, an' put one of you boys on top of him to cover
him up a little, an' talked to the preacher.

"When you got through playin' in the water, he put
clean clothes on you and a clean shirt on himself, an'

by that time I'd begun to get supper. He says: 'It's too hot in here to eat comfortable. Let's have a picnic in the orchard. We'll eat our supper behind the mulberry hedge, under them linden trees.'

"So he carried our supper down, an' a bottle of my wild-grape wine, an' everything tasted good, I can tell you. The wind got cooler as the sun was goin' down, and it turned out pleasant, only I noticed how the leaves was curled up on the linden trees. That made me think, an' I asked your father if that hot wind all day hadn't been terrible hard on the gardens an' the corn.

" 'Corn,' he says, 'there ain't no corn.'

" 'What you talkin' about?' I said. 'Ain't we got forty acres?'

" 'We ain't got an ear,' he says, 'nor nobody else ain't got none. All the corn in this country was cooked by three o'clock today, like you'd roasted it in an oven.'

" 'You mean you won't get no crop at all?' I asked him. I couldn't believe it, after he'd worked so hard.

" 'No crop this year,' he says. 'That's why we're havin' a picnic. We might as well enjoy what we got.'

"An' that's how your father behaved, when all the neighbours was so discouraged they couldn't look you in the face. An' we enjoyed ourselves that year, poor as we was, an' our neighbours wasn't a bit better off for bein' miserable. Some of 'em grieved till they got poor digestions and couldn't relish what they did have."

The younger boys said they thought their father had the best of it. But Rudolph was thinking that, all the same, the neighbours had managed to get ahead more, in the fifteen years since that time. There must be something wrong about his father's way of doing things. He wished he knew what was going on in the back of Polly's mind. He knew she liked his father, but he knew, too, that she was afraid of something. When his mother sent over coffee-cake or prune tarts or a loaf of fresh bread, Polly seemed to regard them with a certain suspicion. When she observed to him that his brothers had nice manners, her tone implied that it was remarkable they should have. With his mother she was stiff and on her guard. Mary's hearty frankness and gusts of good humour irritated her. Polly was afraid of being unusual or conspicuous in any way, of being "ordinary," as she said!

When Mary had finished her story, Rosicky laid aside his pipe.

"You boys like me to tell you about some of dem hard times I been through in London?" Warmly encouraged, he sat rubbing his forehead along the deep creases. It was bothersome to tell a long story in English (he nearly always talked to the boys in Czech), but he wanted Polly to hear this one.

"Well, you know about dat tailor shop I worked in in London? I had one Christmas dere I ain't never forgot. Times was awful bad before Christmas; de boss ain't got much work, an' have it awful hard to pay his rent. It ain't so much fun, bein' poor in a big city like London, I'll say! All de windows is full of good t'ings to eat, an' all de pushcarts in de streets is full, an' you smell 'em all de time, an' you ain't got no money,— not a damn bit. I didn't mind de cold so much, though I didn't have no overcoat, chust a short jacket I'd outgrowed so it wouldn't meet on me, an' my hands was chapped raw. But I always had a good appetite, like you all know, an' de sight of dem pork pies in de windows was awful fur me!

"Day before Christmas was terrible foggy dat year, an' dat fog gits into your bones and makes you all damp like. Mrs. Lifschnitz didn't give us nothin' but a little bread an' drippin' for supper, because she was savin' to try for to give us a good dinner on Christmas Day. After supper de boss say I can go an' enjoy myself, so I went into de streets to listen to de Christmas singers. Dey sing old songs an' make very nice music, an' I run round after dem a good ways, till I got awful hungry. I t'ink maybe if I go home, I can sleep till morning an' forget my belly.

"I went into my corner real quiet, and roll up in my fedder quilt. But I ain't got my head down, till I smell somet'ing good. Seem like it git stronger an' stronger, an' I can't git to sleep noway. I can't understand dat smell. Dere was a gas light in a hall across de court, dat always shine in at my window a little. I got up an' look round. I got a little wooden box in my corner fur a stool, 'cause I ain't got no chair. I picks up dat box, and under it dere is a roast goose on a platter! I can't believe my eyes. I carry it to de window where de light comes in, an' touch it and smell it to find out, an' den I taste it to be sure. I say, I will eat chust one little bite of dat goose, so I can go to sleep, and tomorrow I won't eat none at all. But I tell you, boys, when I stop, one half of dat goose was gone!"

The narrator bowed his head, and the boys shouted. But little Josephine slipped behind his chair and kissed him on the neck beneath his ear.

"Poor little Papa, I don't want him to be hungry!"

"Da's long ago, child. I ain't never been hungry since I had your mudder to cook fur me."

"Go on and tell us the rest, please," said Polly.

"Well, when I come to realize what I done, of course, I felt terrible. I felt better in de stomach, but very bad in de heart. I set on my bed wid dat platter on my knees, an' it all come to me; how hard dat poor woman save to buy dat goose, and how she get some neighbour to cook it dat got more fire, an' how she put it in my corner to keep it away from dem hungry children. Dey was a old carpet hung up to shut my corner off, an' de children wasn't allowed to go in dere. An' I know she put it in my corner because she trust me more'n she did de violin boy. I can't stand it to face her after I spoil de Christmas. So I put on my shoes and go out into de city. I tell myself I better throw myself in de river; but I guess I ain't dat kind of a boy.

"It was after twelve o'clock, an' terrible cold, an' I start out to walk about London all night. I walk along de river awhile, but dey was lots of drunks all along; men, and women too. I chust move along to keep away from de police. I git onto de Strand, an' den over to New Oxford Street, where dere was a big German restaurant on de ground floor, wid big windows all fixed up fine, an' I could see de people havin' parties inside. While I was lookin' in, two men and two ladies come out, laughin' and talkin' and feelin' happy about all dey been eatin' an' drinkin', and dey was speakin' Czech,—not like de Austrians, but like de home folks talk it.

"I guess I went crazy, an' I done what I ain't never done before nor since. I went right up to dem gay people an' begun to beg dem: 'Fellow-countrymen, for God's sake give me money enough to buy a goose!'

"Dey laugh, of course, but de ladies speak awful kind to me, an' dey take me back into de restaurant and give me hot coffee and cakes, an' make me tell all about how I happened to come to London, an' what I was doin' dere. Dey take my name and where I work down on paper, an' both of dem ladies give me ten shillings.

"De big market at Covent Garden ain't very far away, an' by dat time it was open. I go dere an' buy a big goose an' some pork pies, an' potatoes and onions, an' cakes an' oranges fur de children,—all I could carry! When I git home, everybody is still asleep. I pile all I bought on de kitchen table, an' go in an' lay down on my bed, an' I ain't waken up till I hear dat woman scream when she come out into her kitchen. My goodness, but she was surprise! She laugh an' cry at de same time, an' hug me and waken all de children. She ain't stop fur no breakfast; she git de Christmas dinner ready dat morning, and we all sit down an' eat all we can hold. I ain't never seen dat violin boy have all he can hold before.

"Two three days after dat, de two men come to hunt me up, an' dey ask my boss, and he give me a good report an' tell dem I was a steady boy all right. One of dem Bohemians was very smart an' run a Bohemian newspaper in New York, an' de odder was a rich man, in de importing business, an' dey been travelling togedder. Dey told me how t'ings was easier in New York, an' offered to pay my passage when dey was goin' home soon on a boat. My boss say to me: 'You go. You ain't got no chance here, an' I like to see you git ahead, fur you always been a good boy to my woman, and fur dat fine Christmas dinner you give us all.' An' da's how I got to New York."

That night when Rudolph and Polly, arm in arm, were running home across the fields with the bitter wind at their backs, his heart leaped for joy when she said she thought they might have his family come over for supper on New Year's Eve. "Let's get up a nice supper, and not let your mother help at all; make her be company for once."

"That would be lovely of you, Polly," he said humbly. He was a very simple, modest boy, and he, too, felt vaguely that Polly and her sisters were more experienced and worldly than his people.

SIX/   The winter turned out badly for farmers.
It was bitterly cold, and after the first light snows
before Christmas there was no snow at all,—and no
rain. March was as bitter as February. On those days
when the wind fairly punished the country, Rosicky
sat by his window. In the fall he and the boys had
put in a big wheat planting, and now the seed had
frozen in the ground. All that land would have to be
ploughed up and planted over again, planted in corn.
It had happened before, but he was younger then, and
he never worried about what had to be. He was sure
of himself and of Mary; he knew they could bear
what they had to bear, that they would always pull
through somehow. But he was not so sure about the
young ones, and he felt troubled because Rudolph
and Polly were having such a hard start.

Sitting beside his flowering window while the panes
rattled and the wind blew in under the door, Rosicky
gave himself to reflection as he had not done since
those Sundays in the loft of the furniture-factory in
New York, long ago. Then he was trying to find what
he wanted in life for himself; now he was trying to
find what he wanted for his boys, and why it was he
so hungered to feel sure they would be here, working
this very land, after he was gone.

They would have to work hard on the farm, and
probably they would never do much more than make
a living. But if he could think of them as staying here
on the land, he wouldn't have to fear any great un-
kindness for them. Hardships, certainly; it was a hard-
ship to have the wheat freeze in the ground when seed
was so high; and to have to sell your stock because

you had no feed. But there would be other years when everything came along right, and you caught up. And what you had was your own. You didn't have to choose between bosses and strikers, and go wrong either way. You didn't have to do with dishonest and cruel people. They were the only things in his experience he had found terrifying and horrible; the look in the eyes of a dishonest and crafty man, of a scheming and rapacious woman.

In the country, if you had a mean neighbour, you could keep off his land and make him keep off yours. But in the city, all the foulness and misery and brutality of your neighbours was part of your life. The worst things he had come upon in his journey through the world were human,—depraved and poisonous specimens of man. To this day he could recall certain terrible faces in the London streets. There were mean people everywhere, to be sure, even in their own country town here. But they weren't tempered, hardened, sharpened, like the treacherous people in cities who live by grinding or cheating or poisoning their fellow-men. He had helped to bury two of his fellow-workmen in the tailoring trade, and he was distrustful of the organized industries that see one out of the world in big cities. Here, if you were sick, you had Doctor Ed to look after you; and if you died, fat Mr. Haycock, the kindest man in the world, buried you.

It seemed to Rosicky that for good, honest boys like his, the worst they could do on the farm was better than the best they would be likely to do in the city. If he'd had a mean boy, now, one who was crooked and sharp and tried to put anything over on his brothers, then town would be the place for him. But he had no such boy. As for Rudolph, the discontented one, he would give the shirt off his back to anyone who touched his heart. What Rosicky really hoped for his boys was that they could get through the world without ever knowing much about the cruelty of human beings. "Their mother and me ain't prepared them for that," he sometimes said to himself.

These thoughts brought him back to a grateful consideration of his own case. What an escape he had had, to be sure! He, too, in his time, had had to take money for repair work from the hand of a hungry child who let it go so wistfully; because it was money due his boss. And now, in all these years, he had never had to take a cent from any one in bitter need,—never had to look at the face of a woman become like a wolf's from struggle and famine. When he thought of these things, Rosicky would put on his cap and jacket and slip down to the barn and give his work-horses a little extra oats, letting them eat it out of his hand in their slobbery fashion. It was his way of expressing what he felt, and made him chuckle with pleasure.

The spring came warm, with blue skies,—but dry, dry as a bone. The boys began ploughing up the wheat-fields to plant them over in corn. Rosicky would stand at the fence corner and watch them, and the earth was so dry it blew up in clouds of brown dust that hid the horses and the sulky plough and the driver. It was a bad outlook.

The big alfalfa-field that lay between the home place and Rudolph's came up green, but Rosicky was worried because during that open windy winter a great many Russian thistle plants had blown in there and lodged. He kept asking the boys to rake them out; he was afraid their seed would root and "take the alfalfa." Rudolph said that was nonsense. The boys were working so hard planting corn, their father felt he couldn't insist about the thistles, but he set great store by that big alfalfa field. It was a feed you could depend on,—and there was some deeper reason, vague, but strong. The peculiar green of that clover woke early memories in old Rosicky, went back to something in his childhood in the old world. When he was a little boy, he had played in fields of that strong blue-green colour.

One morning, when Rudolph had gone to town in the car, leaving a work-team idle in his barn, Rosicky went over to his son's place, put the horses to the buggy-rake, and set about quietly raking up those thistles. He behaved with guilty caution, and rather enjoyed stealing a march on Doctor Ed, who was just then taking his first vacation in seven years of practice and was attending a clinic in Chicago. Rosicky got the thistles raked up, but did not stop to burn them. That would take some time, and his breath was pretty short, so he thought he had better get the horses back to the barn.

He got them into the barn and to their stalls, but the pain had come on so sharp in his chest that he didn't try to take the harness off. He started for the house, bending lower with every step. The cramp in his chest was shutting him up like a jack-knife. When he reached the windmill, he swayed and caught at the ladder. He saw Polly coming down the hill, running with the swiftness of a slim greyhound. In a flash she had her shoulder under his armpit.

"Lean on me, Father, hard! Don't be afraid. We can get to the house all right."

Somehow they did, though Rosicky became blind with pain; he could keep on his legs, but he couldn't steer his course. The next thing he was conscious of was lying on Polly's bed, and Polly bending over him wringing out bath towels in hot water and putting them on his chest. She stopped only to throw coal into the stove, and she kept the tea-kettle and the black pot going. She put these hot applications on him for nearly an hour, she told him afterwards, and all that time he was drawn up stiff and blue, with the sweat pouring off him.

As the pain gradually loosed its grip, the stiffness went out of his jaws, the black circles round his eyes disappeared, and a little of his natural colour came back. When his daughter-in-law buttoned his shirt over his chest at last, he sighed.

"Da's fine, de way I feel now, Polly. It was a awful bad spell, an' I was so sorry it all come on you like it did."

Polly was flushed and excited. "Is the pain really gone? Can I leave you long enough to telephone over to your place?"

Rosicky's eyelids fluttered. "Don't telephone, Polly. It ain't no use to scare my wife. It's nice and quiet here, an' if I ain't too much trouble to you, just let me lay still till I feel like myself. I ain't got no pain now. It's nice here."

Polly bent over him and wiped the moisture from his face. "Oh, I'm so glad it's over!" she broke out impulsively. "It just broke my heart to see you suffer so, Father."

Rosicky motioned her to sit down on the chair where the tea-kettle had been, and looked up at her with that lively affectionate gleam in his eyes. "You was awful good to me, I won't never forget dat. I hate it to be sick on you like dis. Down at de barn I say to myself, dat young girl ain't had much experience in sickness, I don't want to scare her, an' maybe she's got a baby comin' or somet'ing."

Polly took his hand. He was looking at her so intently and affectionately and confidingly; his eyes seemed to caress her face, to regard it with pleasure. She frowned with her funny streaks of eyebrows, and then smiled back at him.

"I guess maybe there is something of that kind going to happen. But I haven't told anyone yet, not my mother or Rudolph. You'll be the first to know."

His hand pressed hers. She noticed that it was warm again. The twinkle in his yellow-brown eyes seemed to come nearer.

"I like mighty well to see dat little child, Polly," was all he said. Then he closed his eyes and lay half-smiling. But Polly sat still, thinking hard. She had a sudden feeling that nobody in the world, not her mother, not Rudolph, or anyone, really loved her as much as old Rosicky did. It perplexed her. She sat frowning and trying to puzzle it out. It was as if Rosicky had a special gift for loving people, something that was like an ear for music or an eye for colour. It was quiet, unobtrusive; it was merely there. You saw it in his eyes,—perhaps that was why they were merry. You felt it in his hands, too. After he dropped off to sleep, she sat holding his warm, broad, flexible brown hand. She had never seen another in the least like it. She wondered if it wasn't a kind of gypsy hand, it was so alive and quick and light in its communications,—very strange in a farmer. Nearly all the farmers she knew had huge lumps of fists, like mauls, or they were knotty and bony and uncomfortable-looking, with stiff fingers. But Rosicky's was like quicksilver, flexible, muscular, about the colour of a pale cigar, with deep, deep creases across the palm. It wasn't nervous, it wasn't a stupid lump; it was a warm brown human hand, with some cleverness in it, a great deal of generosity, and something else which Polly could only call "gypsy-like,"—something nimble and lively and sure, in the way that animals are.

Polly remembered that hour long afterwards; it had been like an awakening to her. It seemed to her that she had never learned so much about life from anything as from old Rosicky's hand. It brought her to herself; it communicated some direct and untranslatable message.

When she heard Rudolph coming in the car, she ran out to meet him.

"Oh, Rudy, your father's been awful sick! He raked up those thistles he's been worrying about, and afterwards he could hardly get to the house. He suffered so I was afraid he was going to die."

Rudolph jumped to the ground. "Where is he now?"

"On the bed. He's asleep. I was terribly scared, because, you know, I'm so fond of your father." She slipped her arm through his and they went into the house. That afternoon they took Rosicky home and put him to bed, though he protested that he was quite well again.

The next morning he got up and dressed and sat down to breakfast with his family. He told Mary that his coffee tasted better than usual to him, and he warned the boys not to bear any tales to Doctor Ed when he got home. After breakfast he sat down by his window to do some patching and asked Mary to thread several needles for him before she went to feed her chickens,—her eyes were better than his, and her hands steadier. He lit his pipe and took up John's overalls. Mary had been watching him anxiously all morning, and as she went out of the door with her bucket of scraps, she saw that he was smiling. He was thinking, indeed, about Polly, and how he might never have known what a tender heart she had if he hadn't got sick over there. Girls nowadays didn't wear their heart on their sleeve. But now he knew Polly would make a fine woman after the foolishness wore off. Either a woman had that sweetness at her heart or she hadn't. You couldn't always tell by the look of them; but if they had that, everything came out right in the end.

After he had taken a few stitches, the cramp began in his chest, like yesterday. He put his pipe cautiously down on the window-sill and bent over to ease the pull. No use,—he had better try to get to his bed if he could. He rose and groped his way across the familiar floor, which was rising and falling like the deck of a ship. At the door he fell. When Mary came in, she found him lying there, and the moment she touched him she knew that he was gone.

Doctor Ed was away when Rosicky died, and for the first few weeks after he got home he was hard driven. Every day he said to himself that he must get out to see that family that had lost their father. One soft, warm moonlight night in early summer he started for the farm. His mind was on other things, and not until his road ran by the grave-yard did he realize that Rosicky wasn't over there on the hill where the red lamplight shone, but here, in the moonlight. He stopped his car, shut off the engine, and sat there for a while.

A sudden hush had fallen on his soul. Everything here seemed strangely moving and significant, though signifying what, he did not know. Close by the wire fence stood Rosicky's mowing-machine, where one of the boys had been cutting hay that afternoon; his own work-horses had been going up and down there. The new-cut hay perfumed all the night air. The moonlight silvered the long, billowy grass that grew over the graves and hid the fence; the few little evergreens stood out black in it, like shadows in a pool. The sky was very blue and soft, the stars rather faint because the moon was full.

For the first time it struck Doctor Ed that this was really a beautiful graveyard. He thought of city cemeteries; acres of shrubbery and heavy stone, so arranged and lonely and unlike anything in the living world. Cities of the dead, indeed; cities of the forgotten, of the "put away." But this was open and free, this little square of long grass which the wind for ever stirred. Nothing but the sky overhead, and the many-coloured fields running on until they met that sky. The horses worked here in summer; the neighbours passed on their way to town; and over yonder, in the cornfield, Rosicky's own cattle would be eating fodder as winter came on. Nothing could be more undeathlike than this place; nothing could be more right for a man who had helped to do the work of great cities and had always longed for the open country and had got to it at last. Rosicky's life seemed to him complete and beautiful.

New York, 1928

The Best Years*

ONE / On a bright September morning in the year 1899 Miss Evangeline Knightly was driving through the beautiful Nebraska land which lies between the Platte River and the Kansas line. She drove slowly, for she loved the country, and she held the reins loosely in her gloved hand. She drove about a great deal and always wore leather gauntlets. Her hands were small, well shaped and very white, but they freckled in hot sunlight.

Miss Knightly was a charming person to meet —and an unusual type in a new country: oval face, small head delicately set (the oval chin tilting inward instead of the square chin thrust out), hazel eyes, a little blue, a little green, tiny dots of brown. . . . Somehow these splashes of colour made light—and warmth. When she laughed, her eyes positively glowed with humour, and in each oval cheek a roguish dimple came magically to the surface. Her laugh

* From *The Old Beauty and Others*, 1948. This was the last story that Willa Cather completed.

was delightful because it was intelligent, discriminating, not the physical spasm which seizes children when they are tickled, and growing boys and girls when they are embarrassed. When Miss Knightly laughed, it was apt to be because of some happy coincidence or droll mistake. The farmers along the road always felt flattered if they could make Miss Knightly laugh. Her voice had as many colours as her eyes—nearly always on the bright side, though it had a beautiful gravity for people who were in trouble.

It is only fair to say that in the community where she lived Miss Knightly was considered an intelligent young woman, but plain—distinctly plain. The standard of female beauty seems to be the same in all newly settled countries: Australia, New Zealand, the farming country along the Platte. It is, and was, the glowing, smiling calendar girl sent out to advertise agricultural implements. Colour was everything, modelling was nothing. A nose was a nose—any shape would do; a forehead was the place where the hair stopped, chin utterly negligible unless it happened to be more than two inches long.

Miss Knightly's old mare, Molly, took her time along the dusty, sunflower-bordered roads that morning, occasionally pausing long enough to snatch off a juicy, leafy sunflower top in her yellow teeth. This she munched as she ambled along. Although Molly had almost the slowest trot in the world, she really preferred walking. Sometimes she fell into a doze and stumbled. Miss Knightly also, when she was abroad on these long drives, preferred the leisurely pace. She loved the beautiful autumn country; loved to look at it, to breathe it. She was not a "dreamy" person, but she was thoughtful and very observing. She relished the morning; the great blue of the sky, smiling, cloudless,—and the land that lay level as far as the eye could see. The horizon was like a perfect circle, a great embrace, and within it lay the cornfields, still green, and the yellow wheat stubble, miles and miles of it, and the pasture lands where the white-faced cattle led lives of utter content. All their movements were deliberate and dignified. They grazed through all the morning; approached their metal water tank and drank. If the windmill had run too long and the tank had overflowed, the cattle trampled the overflow into deep mud and cooled their feet. Then they drifted off to graze again. Grazing was not merely eating, it was also a pastime, a form of reflection, perhaps meditation.

Miss Knightly was thinking, as Molly jogged along, that the barbed-wire fences, though ugly in themselves, had their advantages. They did not cut the country up into patterns as did the rail fences and stone walls of her native New England. They were, broadly regarded, invisible—did not impose themselves upon the eye. She seemed to be driving through a fineless land. On her left the Hereford cattle apparently wandered at will: the tall sunflowers hid the wire that kept them off the road. Far away, on the horizon line, a troop of colts were galloping, all in the same direction—purely for exercise, one would say. Between her and the horizon the white wheels of windmills told her where the farmhouses sat.

Miss Knightly was abroad this morning with a special purpose—to visit country schools. She was the County Superintendent of Public Instruction. A grim title, that, to put upon a charming young woman. . . . Fortunately it was seldom used except on reports which she signed, and there it was usually printed. She was not even called "the Superintendent." A country schoolteacher said to her pupils: "I think Miss Knightly will come to see us this week. She was at Walnut Creek yesterday."

After she had driven westward through the pasture lands for an hour or so, Miss Knightly turned her mare north and very soon came into a rich farming district, where the fields were too valuable to be used for much grazing. Big red barns, rows of yellow straw stacks, green orchards, trim white farmhouses, fenced gardens.

Looking at her watch, Miss Knightly found that it was already after eleven o'clock. She touched Molly delicately with the whip and roused her to a jog trot. Presently they stopped before a little one-storey schoolhouse. All the windows were open. At the hitch-bar in the yard five horses were tethered— their saddles and bridles piled in an empty buck-board. There was a yard, but no fence—though on one side of the playground was a woven-wire fence covered with the vines of sturdy rambler roses—very pretty in the spring. It enclosed a cemetery—very few graves, very much sun and waving yellow grass, open to the singing from the schoolroom and the shouts of the boys playing ball at noon. The cemetery never depressed the children, and surely the school cast no gloom over the cemetery.

When Miss Knightly stopped before the door, a boy ran out to hand her from the buggy and to take care of Molly. The little teacher stood on the doorstep, her face lost, as it were, in a wide smile of tremulous gladness.

Miss Knightly took her hand, held it for a moment and looked down into the child's face—she was scarcely more—and said in the very gentlest shade of her many-shaded voice, "Everything going well, Lesley?"

The teacher replied in happy little gasps, "Oh yes, Miss Knightly! It's all so much easier than it was last year. I have some such lovely children— and they're all *good!*"

Miss Knightly took her arm, and they went into the schoolroom. The pupils grinned a welcome to the visitor. The teacher asked the conventional question: What recitation would she like to hear?

Whatever came next in the usual order, Miss Knightly said.

The class in geography came next. The children were "bounding" the States. When the North Atlantic States had been disposed of with more or less accuracy, the little teacher said they would now jump to the Middle West, to bring the lesson nearer home.

"Suppose we begin with Illinois. That is your State, Edward, so I will call on you."

A pale boy rose and came front of the class; a little fellow aged ten, maybe, who was plainly a newcomer—wore knee pants and stockings, instead of long trousers or blue overalls like the other boys. His hands were clenched at his sides, and he was evidently much frightened. Looking appealingly at the little teacher, he began in a high treble: "The State of Illinois is bounded on the north by Lake Michigan, on the east by Lake Michigan . . ." He felt he had gone astray, and language utterly failed. A quick shudder ran over him from head to foot, and an accident happened. His dark blue stockings grew darker still, and his knickerbockers very dark. He stood there as if nailed to the floor. The teacher went up to him and took his hand and led him to his desk.

"You're too tired, Edward," she said. "We're all tired, and it's almost noon. So you can all run out and play, while I talk to Miss Knightly and tell her how naughty you all are."

The children laughed (all but poor Edward), laughed heartily, as if they were suddenly relieved from some strain. Still laughing and punching each other they ran out into the sunshine.

Miss Knightly and the teacher (her name, by the way, was Lesley Ferguesson) sat down on a bench in the corner.

"I'm so sorry that happened, Miss Knightly. I oughtn't to have called on him. He's so new here, and he's a nervous little boy. I thought he'd like to speak up for his State. He seems homesick."

"My dear, I'm glad you did call on him, and I'm glad the poor little fellow had an accident,—if he doesn't get too much misery out of it. The way those children behaved astonished me. Not a wink, or grin, or even a look. Not a wink from the Haymaker boy. I watched him. His mother has no such delicacy. They have just the best kind of good manners. How do you do it, Lesley?"

Lesley gave a happy giggle and flushed as red as a poppy. "Oh, I don't do anything! You see they really *are* nice children. You remember last year I did have a little trouble—till they got used to me."

"But they all passed their finals, and one girl, who was older than her teacher, got a school."

"Hush, hush, ma'am! I'm afraid for the walls to hear it! Nobody knows our secret but my mother."

"I'm very well satisfied with the results of our crime, Lesley."

The girl blushed again. She loved to hear Miss Knightly speak her name, because she always sounded the *s* like a *z*, which made it seem gentler and more intimate. Nearly everyone else, even her mother, hissed the *s* as if it were spelled "Lessley." It was embarrassing to have such a queer name, but she respected it because her father had chosen it for her.

"Where are you going to stay all night, Miss Knightly?" she asked rather timidly.

"I think Mrs. Ericson expects me to stay with her."

"Mrs. Hunt, where I stay, would be awful glad

to have you, but I know you'll be more comfortable at Mrs. Ericson's. She's a lovely housekeeper." Lesley resigned the faint hope that Miss Knightly would stay where she herself boarded, and broke out eagerly:

"Oh, Miss Knightly, have you seen any of our boys lately? Mother's too busy to write to me often."

"Hector looked in at my office last week. He came to the Court House with a telegram for the sheriff. He seemed well and happy."

"Did he? But Miss Knightly, I wish he hadn't taken that messenger job. I hate so for him to quit school."

"Now, I wouldn't worry about that, my dear. School isn't everything. He'll be getting good experience every day at the depot."

"Do you think so? I haven't seen him since he went to work."

"Why, how long has it been since you were home?"

"It's over a month now. Not since my school started. Father has been working all our horses on the farm. Maybe you can share my lunch with me?"

"I brought a lunch for the two of us, my dear. Call your favourite boy to go to my buggy and get my basket for us. After lunch I would like to hear the advanced arithmetic class."

While the pupils were doing their sums at the blackboard, Miss Knightly herself was doing a little figuring. This was Thursday. Tomorrow she would visit two schools, and she had planned to spend Friday night with a pleasant family on Farmers' Creek. But she could change her schedule and give this homesick child a visit with her family in the county seat. It would inconvenience her very little.

When the class in advanced arithmetic was dismissed, Miss Knightly made a joking little talk to the children and told them about a very bright little girl in Scotland who knew nearly a whole play of Shakespeare's by heart, but who wrote in her diary: "Nine times nine is the Devil"; which proved, she said, that there are two kinds of memory, and God is very good to anyone to whom he gives both kinds. Then she asked if the pupils might have a special recess of half an hour, as a present from her. They gave her a cheer and out they trooped, the boys to the ball ground, and the girls to the cemetery, to sit neatly on the headstones and discuss Miss Knightly.

During their recess the Superintendent disclosed her plan. "I've been wondering, Lesley, whether you wouldn't like to go back to town with me after school tomorrow. We could get into MacAlpin by seven o'clock, and you could have all of Saturday and Sunday at home. Then we would make an early start Monday morning, and I would drop you here at the schoolhouse at nine o'clock."

The little teacher caught her breath—she became quite pale for a moment.

"Oh Miss Knightly, could you? Could you?"

"Of course I can. I'll stop for you here at four o'clock tomorrow afternoon."

TWO / The dark secret between Lesley and Miss Knightly was that only this September had the girl reached the legal age for teachers, yet she had been teaching all last year when she was still under age!

Last summer, when the applicants for teachers' certificates took written examinations in the County Superintendent's offices at the Court House in Mac-Alpin, Lesley Ferguesson had appeared with some twenty-six girls and nine boys. She wrote all morning and all afternoon for two days. Miss Knightly found her paper one of the best in the lot. A week later, when all the papers were filed, Miss Knightly told Lesley she could certainly give her a school. The morning after she had thus notified Lesley, she found the girl herself waiting on the sidewalk in front of the house where Miss Knightly boarded.

"Could I walk over to the Court House with you, Miss Knightly? I ought to tell you something," she blurted out at once. "On that paper I didn't put down my real age. I put down sixteen, and I won't be fifteen until this September."

"But I checked you with the high-school records, Lesley."

"I know. I put it down wrong there, too. I didn't want to be the class baby, and I hoped I could get a school soon, to help out at home."

The County Superintendent thought she would long remember that walk to the Court House. She could see that the child had spent a bad night; and she had walked up from her home down by the depot, quite a mile away, probably without breakfast.

"If your age is wrong on both records, why do you tell me about it now?"

"Oh, Miss Knightly, I got to thinking about it last night, how if you did give me a school it might all come out, and mean people would say you knew about it and broke the law."

Miss Knightly was thoughtless enough to chuckle. "But, my dear, don't you see that if I didn't know about it until this moment, I am completely innocent?"

The child who was walking beside her stopped short and burst into sobs. Miss Knightly put her arm around those thin, eager, forward-reaching shoulders.

"Don't cry, dear. I was only joking. There's nothing very dreadful about it. You didn't give your age under oath, you know." The sobs didn't stop. "Listen, let me tell you something. That big Hatch boy put his age down as nineteen, and I know he was teaching down in Nemaha County four years ago. I can't always be sure about the age applicants put down. I have to use my judgment."

The girl lifted her pale, troubled face and murmured, "Judgment?"

"Yes. Some girls are older at thirteen than others are at eighteen. Your paper was one of the best handed in this year, and I am going to give you a school. Not a big one, but a nice one, in a nice part of the county. Now let's go into Ernie's coffee shop and have some more breakfast. You have a long walk home."

Of course, fourteen was rather young for a teacher in an ungraded school, where she was likely to have pupils of sixteen and eighteen in her classes. But Miss Knightly's "judgment" was justified by the fact that in June the school directors of the Wild Rose district asked to have "Miss Ferguesson" back for the following year.

THREE / At four o'clock on Friday afternoon Miss Knightly stopped at the Wild Rose schoolhouse to find the teacher waiting by the roadside, and the pupils already scattering across the fields, their tin lunch pails flashing back the sun. Lesley was standing almost in the road itself, her grey "telescope" bag at her feet. The moment old Molly stopped, she stowed her bag in the back of the buggy and climbed in beside Miss Knightly. Her smile was so eager and happy that her friend chuckled softly. "You still get a little homesick, don't you, Lesley?"

She didn't deny it. She gave a guilty laugh and murmured, "I do miss the boys."

The afternoon sun was behind them, throwing over the pastures and the harvested, resting fields that wonderful light, so yellow that it is actually orange. The three hours and the fourteen miles seemed not overlong. As the buggy neared the town of MacAlpin, Miss Knightly thought she could feel, Lesley's heart beat. The girl had been silent a long while when she exclaimed:

"Look, there's the standpipe!"

The object of this emotion was a red sheet-iron tube which thrust its naked ugliness some eighty feet into the air and held the water supply for the town of MacAlpin. As it stood on a hill, it was the first thing one saw on approaching the town from the west. Old Molly, too, seemed to have spied this heartening landmark, for she quickened her trot without encouragement from the whip. From that point on, Lesley said not a word. There were two more low hills (very low), and then Miss Knightly turned off the main road and drove by a short cut through the baseball ground, to the south appendix of the town proper, the "depot settlement" where the Ferguessons lived.

Their house stood on a steep hillside—a storey-and-a-half frame house with a basement on the downhill side, faced with brick up to the first-floor level. When the buggy stopped before the yard gate, two little boys came running out of the front door. Miss Knightly's passenger vanished from her side—she didn't know just when Lesley alighted. Her attention was distracted by the appearance of the mother, with a third boy, still in kilts, trotting behind her.

Mrs. Ferguesson was not a person who could be overlooked. All the merchants in MacAlpin admitted that she was a fine figure of a woman. As she came down the little yard and out of the gate, the evening breeze ruffled her wavy auburn hair. Her quick step and alert, upright carriage gave one the impression that she got things done. Coming up to the buggy, she took Miss Knightly's hand.

"Why, it's Miss Knightly! And she's brought our girl along to visit us. That was mighty clever of you, Miss, and these boys will surely be a happy family. They do miss their sister." She spoke clearly, distinctly, but with a slight Missouri turn of speech.

By this time Lesley and her brothers had become telepathically one. Miss Knightly couldn't tell what the boys said to her, or whether they said anything, but they had her old canvas bag out of the buggy and up on the porch in no time at all. Lesley ran toward the front door, hurried back to thank Miss Knightly, and then disappeared, holding fast to the little chap in skirts. She had forgotten to ask at what time Miss Knightly would call for her on Monday, but her mother attended to that. When Mrs. Ferguesson followed the children through the hall and the little back parlour into the dining-room, Lesley turned to her and asked breathlessly, almost sharply:

"Where's Hector?"

"He's often late on Friday night, dear. He telephoned me from the depot and said not to wait supper for him—he'd get a sandwich at the lunch counter. Now how *are* you, my girl?" Mrs. Ferguesson put her hands on Lesley's shoulders and looked into her glowing eyes.

"Just fine, Mother. I like my school so much! And the scholars are nicer even than they were last year. I just love some of them."

At this the little boy in kilts (the fashion of the times, though he was four years old) caught his sister's skirt in his two hands and jerked it to get her attention. "No, no!" he said mournfully, "you don't love anybody but us!"

His mother laughed, and Lesley stooped and gave him the tight hug he wanted.

The family supper was over. Mrs. Ferguesson put on her apron. "Sit right down, Lesley, and talk to the children. No, I won't let you help me. You'll help me most by keeping them out of my way. I'll scramble you an egg and fry you some ham, so sit right down in your own place. I have some stewed plums for your dessert, and a beautiful angel cake I bought at the Methodist bake sale. Your father's gone to some political meeting, so we had supper early. You'll be a nice surprise for him when he gets home. He hadn't been gone half an hour when Miss Knightly drove up. Sit still, dear, it only bothers me if anybody tries to help me. I'll let you wash the dishes afterward, like we always do."

Lesley sat down at the half-cleared table; an oval-shaped table which could be extended by the insertion of "leaves" when Mrs. Ferguesson had company. The room was already dusky (twilights are short in a flat country), and one of the boys switched on the light which hung by a cord high above the table. A shallow china shade over the bulb threw a glaring white light down on the sister and the boys who stood about her chair. Lesley wrinkled up her brow, but it didn't occur to her that the light was too strong. She gave herself up to the feeling of being at home. It went all through her, that feeling, like getting into a warm bath when one is tired. She was safe from everything, was where she wanted to be, where she ought to be. A plant that has been washed out by a rain storm feels like that, when a kind gardener puts it gently back into its own earth with its own group.

The two older boys, Homer and Vincent, kept interrupting each other, trying to tell her things, but she didn't really listen to what they said. The little fellow stood close beside her chair, holding on to her skirt, fingering the glass buttons on her jacket. He was named Bryan, for his father's hero, but he didn't fit the name very well. He was a rather wistful and timid child.

Mrs. Ferguesson brought the ham and eggs and the warmed-up coffee. Then she sat down opposite her daughter to watch her enjoy her supper. "Now don't talk to her, boys. Let her eat in peace."

Vincent spoke up. "Can't I just tell her what happened to my lame pigeon?"

Mrs. Ferguesson merely shook her head. She had control in that household, sure enough!

Before Lesley had quite finished her supper she heard the front door open and shut. The boys started up, but the mother raised a warning finger. They understood; a surprise. They were still as mice, and listened: A pause in the hall . . . he was hanging up his cap. Then he came in—the flower of the family.

For a moment he stood speechless in the doorway, the "incandescent" glaring full on his curly yellow hair and his amazed blue eyes. He was surprised indeed!

"Lesley!" he breathed, as if he were talking in his sleep.

She couldn't sit still. Without knowing that she got up and took a step, she had her arms around her brother. "It's me, Hector! Ain't I lucky? Miss Knightly brought me in."

"What time did you get here? You might have telephoned me, Mother."

"Dear, she ain't been here much more than half an hour."

"And Miss Knightly brought you in with old Molly, did she?" Oh, the lovely voice he had, that Hector!—warm, deliberate . . . it made the most commonplace remark full of meaning. He had to say merely that—and it told his appreciation of Miss

Knightly's kindness, even a playful gratitude to Molly, her clumsy, fat, road-pounding old mare. He was tall for his age, was Hector, and he had the fair pink-cheeked complexion which Lesley should have had and didn't.

Mrs. Ferguesson rose. "Now let's all go into the parlour and talk. We'll come back and clear up afterward." With this she opened the folding doors, and they followed her and found comfortable chairs —there was even a home-made hassock for Bryan. There were real books in the sectional bookcases (old Ferg's fault), and there was a real Brussels carpet in soft colours on the floor. That was Lesley's fault. Most of her savings from her first year's teaching had gone into that carpet. She had chosen it herself from the samples which Marshall Field's travelling man brought to MacAlpin. There were comfortable old-fashioned pictures on the walls—"Venice by Moonlight" and such. Lesley and Hector thought it a beautiful room.

Of course the room was pleasant because of the feeling the children had for one another, and because in Mrs. Ferguesson there was authority and organization. Here the family sat and talked until Father came home. He was always treated a little like company. His wife and his children had a deep respect for him and for experimental farming, and profound veneration for William Jennings Bryan. Even little Bryan knew he was named for a great man, and must some day stop being afraid of the dark.

James Grahame Ferguesson was a farmer. He spent most of his time on what he called an "experimental farm." (The neighbours had other names for it— some of them amusing.) He was a loosely built man; had drooping shoulders carried with a forward thrust. He was a ready speaker, and usually made the Fourth of July speech in MacAlpin—spoke from a platform in the Court House grove, and even the farmers who joked about Ferguesson came to hear him. Alf Delaney declared: "I like to see anything done well—even talking. If old Ferg could shuck corn as fast as he can rustle the dictionary, I'd hire him, even if he is a Pop."

Old Ferg was not at all old—just turned forty —but he was fussy about the spelling of his name. He wrote it James Ferguesson. The merchants, even the local newspaper, simply would not spell it that way. They left letters out, or they put letters in. He complained about this repeatedly, and the result was that he was simply called "Ferg" to his face, and "old Ferg" to his back. His neighbours, both in town and in the country where he farmed, liked him because he gave them so much to talk about. He couldn't keep a hired man long at any wages. His habits were too unconventional. He rose early, saw to the chores like any other man, and went into the field for the morning. His lunch was a cold spread from his wife's kitchen, reinforced by hot tea. (The hired man was expected to bring his own lunch—outrageous!) After lunch Mr. Ferguesson took off his boots and lay down on the blue gingham sheets of a wide bed, and remained there until what he called "the cool of the afternoon." When that refreshing season arrived, he fed and watered his work horses, put the young gelding to his buckboard, and drove four miles to MacAlpin for his wife's hot supper. Mrs. Ferguesson, though not at all a meek woman or a stupid one, unquestioningly believed him when he told her that he did his best thinking in the afternoon. He hinted to her that he was working out in his head something that would benefit the farmers of the county more than all the corn and wheat they could raise even in a good year.

Sometimes Ferguesson did things she regretted—not because they were wrong, but because other people had mean tongues. When a fashion came in for giving names to farms which had hitherto been designated by figures (range, section, quarter, etc.), and his neighbours came out with "Lone Tree Farm," "Cold Spring Farm," etc., Ferguesson tacked on a cottonwood tree by his gate a neatly painted board inscribed: Wide Awake Farm.

His neighbours, who could never get used to his afternoon siesta, were not long in converting this prophetic christening into "Hush-a-bye Farm." Mrs. Ferguesson overheard some of this joking on a Saturday night (she was marketing late after a lodge meeting on top of a busy day), and she didn't like it. On Sunday morning when he was dressing for church, she asked her husband why he ever gave the farm such a foolish name. He explained to her that the important crop on that farm was an idea. His farm was like an observatory where one watched the signs of the times and saw the great change that was coming for the benefit of all mankind. He even quoted Tennyson about looking into the future "far as human eye could see." It had been a long time since he had quoted any poetry to her. She sighed and dropped the matter.

On the whole, Ferg did himself a good turn when he put up that piece of nomenclature. People drove out of their way for miles to see it. They felt more kindly toward old Ferg because he wrote himself down such an ass. In a hard-working farming community a good joke is worth something. Ferguesson himself felt a gradual warming toward him among his neighbours. He ascribed it to the power of his oratory. It was really because he had made himself so absurd, but this he never guessed. Idealists are seldom afraid of ridicule—if they recognize it.

The Ferguesson children believed that their father was misunderstood by people of inferior intelligence, and that conviction gave them a "cause" which bound them together. They must do better than other children; better in school, and better on the playground. They must turn in a quarter of a dollar to help their mother out whenever they could. Experimental farming wasn't immediately remunerative.

Fortunately there was never any rent to pay. They owned their house down by the depot. When Mrs. Ferguesson's father died down in Missouri, she bought that place with what he left her. She knew that was the safe thing to do, her husband being a thinker. Her children were bound to her, and to that house, by the deepest, the most solemn loyalty. They never spoke of that covenant to each other, never even formulated it in their own minds—never. It was a consciousness they shared, and it gave them a family complexion.

On this Saturday of Lesley's surprise visit home, Father was with the family for breakfast. That was always a pleasant way to begin the day—especially on Saturday, when no one was in a hurry. He had grave good manners toward his wife and his children. He talked to them as if they were grown-up, reasonable beings—talked a trifle as if from a rostrum, perhaps,—and he never indulged in small-town gossip. He was much more likely to tell them what he had read in the *Omaha World-Herald* yesterday; news of the State capital and the national capital. Sometimes he told them what a grasping, selfish country England was. Very often he explained to them how the gold standard had kept the poor man down. The family seldom bothered him about petty matters—such as that Homer needed new shoes, or that the iceman's bill for the whole summer had come in for the third time. Mother would take care of that.

On this particular Saturday morning Ferguesson gave especial attention to Lesley. He asked her about her school, and had her name her pupils. "I think you are fortunate to have the Wild Rose school, Lesley," he said as he rose from the table. "The farmers up there are open-minded and prosperous. I have sometimes wished that I had settled up there, though there are certain advantages in living at the county seat. The educational opportunities are better. Your friendship with Miss Knightly has been a broadening influence."

He went out to hitch up the buckboard to drive to the farm, while his wife put up the lunch he was to take along with him, and Lesley went upstairs to make the beds.

"Upstairs" was a story in itself, a secret romance. No caller or neighbour had ever been allowed to go up there. All the children loved it—it was their very own world where there were no older people poking about to spoil things. And it was unique—not at all like other people's upstairs chambers. In her stuffy little bedroom out in the country Lesley had more than once cried for it.

Lesley and the boys liked space, not tight cubby-holes. Their upstairs was a long attic which ran the whole length of the house, from the front door down-stairs to the kitchen at the back. Its great charm was that it was unlined. No plaster, no beaver-board lining; just the roof shingles, supported by long, un-planed, splintery rafters that sloped from the sharp roof-peak down to the floor of the attic. Bracing these long roof rafters were cross rafters on which one could hang things—a little personal washing, a curtain for tableaux, a rope swing for Bryan.

In this spacious, undivided loft were two brick chimneys, going up in neat little stair-steps from the plank floor to the shingle roof—and out of it to the stars! The chimneys were of red, unglazed brick, with lines of white mortar to hold them together.

Last year, after Lesley first got her school, Mrs. Ferguesson exerted her authority and partitioned off a little room over the kitchen end of the "upstairs" for her daughter. Before that, all the children slept in this delightful attic. The three older boys occupied two wide beds, their sister her little single bed. Bryan, subject to croup, still slumbered downstairs near his mother, but he looked forward to his ascension as to a state of pure beatitude.

There was certainly room enough up there for widely scattered quarters, but the three beds stood in a row, as in a hospital ward. The children liked to be close enough together to share experiences.

Experiences were many. Perhaps the most exciting was when the driving, sleety snowstorms came on winter nights. The roof shingles were old and had curled under hot summer suns. In a driving snowstorm the frozen flakes sifted in through all those little cracks, sprinkled the beds and the children, melted on their faces, in their hair! That was delightful. The rest of you was snug and warm under blankets and comforters, with a hot brick at one's feet. The wind howled outside; sometimes the white light from the snow and the half-strangled moon came in through the single end window. Each child had his own dream-adventure. They did not exchange confidences; every "fellow" had a right to his own. They never told their love.

If they turned in early, they had a good while to enjoy the outside weather; they never went to sleep until after ten o'clock, for then came the sweetest morsel of the night. At that hour Number Seventeen, the westbound passenger, whistled in. The station and the engine house were perhaps an eighth of a mile down the hill, and from far away across

the meadows the children could hear that whistle.
Then came the heavy pants of the locomotive in
the frosty air. Then a hissing—then silence: she was
taking water.

On Saturdays the children were allowed to go
down to the depot to see Seventeen come in. It
was a fine sight on winter nights. Sometimes the
great locomotive used to sweep in armoured in ice
and snow, breathing fire like a dragon, its great red
eye shooting a blinding beam along the white road-
bed and shining wet rails. When it stopped, it panted
like a great beast. After it was watered by the big
hose from the overhead tank, it seemed to draw long
deep breaths, ready to charge afresh over the great
Western land.

Yes, they were grand old warriors, those towering locomotives of other days. They seemed to mean
power, conquest, triumph—Jim Hill's dream. They
set children's hearts beating from Chicago to Los
Angeles. They were the awakeners of many a dream.

As she made the boys' beds that Saturday morning
and put on clean sheets, Lesley was thinking she
would give a great deal to sleep out here as she used
to. But when she got her school last year, her mother
had said she must have a room of her own. So a
carpenter brought sheathing and "lined" the end of
the long loft—the end over the kitchen; and Mrs.
Ferguesson bought a little yellow washstand and a
bowl and pitcher, and said with satisfaction: "Now
you see, Lesley, if you were sick, we would have
some place to take the doctor." To be sure, the
doctor would have to be admitted through the kitchen,
and then come up a dark winding stairway with two
turns. (Mr. Ferguesson termed it "the turnpike."
His old Scotch grandmother, he said, had always

thus called a winding stairway.) And Lesley's room, when you got there, was very like a snug wooden box. It was possible, of course, to leave her door open into the long loft, where the wood was brown and the chimneys red and the weather always so close to one. Out there things were still wild and rough—it wasn't a bedroom or a chamber—it was a hall, in the old baronial sense, reminded her of the lines in their *Grimm's Fairy Tales* book:

> Return, return, thou youthful bride,
> This is a robbers' hall inside.

FOUR/   When her daughter had put the attic to rights, Mrs. Ferguesson went uptown to do her Saturday marketing. Lesley slipped out through the kitchen door and sat down on the back porch. The front porch was kept neat and fit to receive callers, but the back porch was given over to the boys. It was a messy-looking place, to be sure. From the wooden ceiling hung two trapezes. At one corner four boxing gloves were piled in a broken chair. In the trampled, grassless back yard, two-by-fours, planted upright, supported a length of lead pipe on which Homer practised bar exercises. Lesley sat down on the porch floor, her feet on the ground, and sank into idleness and safety and perfect love.

The boys were much the dearest things in the world to her. To love them so much was just . . . happiness. To think about them was the most perfect form of happiness. Had they been actually present, swinging on the two trapezes, turning on the bar, she would have been too much excited, too actively happy to be perfectly happy. But sitting in the warm sun, with her feet on the good ground, even her mother away, she almost ceased to exist. The feeling of being at home was complete, absolute: it made her sleepy. And that feeling was not so much the sense of being protected by her father and mother as of being with, and being one with, her brothers. It was the clan feeling, which meant life or death for the blood, not for the individual. For some reason, or for no reason, back in the beginning, creatures wanted the blood to continue.

After the noonday dinner Mrs. Ferguesson thoughtfully confided to her daughter while they were washing the dishes:

"Lesley, I'm divided in my mind. I would so appreciate a quiet afternoon with you, but I've a sort of engagement with the P.E.O. A lady from Canada is to be there to talk to us, and I've promised to introduce her. And just when I want to have a quiet time with you."

Lesley gave a sigh of relief and thought how fortunate it is that circumstances do sometimes make up our mind for us. In that battered canvas bag upstairs there was a roll of arithmetic papers and "essays" which hung over her like a threat. Now she would have a still hour in their beautiful parlour to correct them; the shades drawn down, just enough light to read by, her father's unabridged at hand, and the boys playing bat and pitch in the back yard.

Lesley and her brothers were proud of their mother's good looks, and that she never allowed herself to become a household drudge, as so many of her neighbours did. She "managed," and the boys helped her to manage. For one thing, there were never any dreary tubs full of washing standing about, and there was no ironing day to make a hole in the week. They sent all the washing, even the sheets, to the town steam laundry. Hector, with his weekly wages as messenger boy, and Homer and Vincent with their stable jobs, paid for it. That simple expedient did away with the worst blight of the working man's home.

Mrs. Ferguesson was "public-spirited," and she was the friend of all good causes. The business men of the town agreed that she had a great deal of influence, and that her name added strength to any committee. She was generally spoken of as a very *practical* woman, with an emphasis which implied several things. She was a "joiner," too! She was a Royal Neighbor, and a Neighborly Neighbor, and a P.E.O., and an Eastern Star. She had even joined the Methodist Win-a-Couple, though she warned them that she could not attend their meetings, as she liked to spend some of her evenings at home.

Promptly at six thirty Monday morning Miss Knightly's old mare stopped in front of the Ferguessons' house. The four boys were all on the front porch. James himself carried Lesley's bag down and put it into the buggy. He thanked the Superintendent very courteously for her kindness and kissed his daughter good-bye.

It had been at no trifling sacrifice that Miss Knightly was able to call for Lesley at six thirty. Customarily she started on her long drives at nine o'clock. This morning she had to give an extra half-dollar to the man who came to curry and harness her mare. She herself got no proper breakfast, but a cold sandwich and a cup of coffee at the station lunch counter—the only eating-place open at six o'clock. Most serious of all, she must push Molly a little on the road, to land her passenger at the Wild Rose schoolhouse at nine o'clock. Such small inconveniences do not sum up to an imposing total, but we assume them only for persons we really care for.

FIVE / It was Christmas Eve. The town was busy with Christmas "exercises," and all the churches were lit up. Hector Ferguesson was going slowly up the hill which separated the depot settlement from the town proper. He walked at no messenger-boy pace tonight, crunching under his feet the snow which had fallen three days ago, melted, and then frozen hard. His hands were in the pockets of his new overcoat, which was so long that it almost touched the ground when he toiled up the steepest part of the hill. It was very heavy and not very warm. In those days there was a theory that in topcoats very little wool was necessary if they were woven tight enough and hard enough to "keep out the cold." A barricade was the idea. Hector carried the weight and clumsiness bravely, proudly. His new overcoat was a Christmas present from his sister. She had gone to the big town in the next county to shop for it, and bought it with her own money. He was thinking how kind Lesley was, and how hard she had worked for that money, and how much she had to put up with in the rough farmhouse where she boarded, out in the country. It was usually a poor housekeeper who was willing to keep a teacher, since they paid so little. Probably the amount Lesley spent for that coat would have kept her at a comfortable house all winter. When he grew up, and made lots of money (a brakeman—maybe an engineer), he would certainly be good to his sister.

Hector was a strange boy; a blend of the soft and the hard. In action he was practical, executive, like his mother. But in his mind, in his thoughts and plans, he was extravagant, often absurd. His mother suspected that he was "dreamy." Tonight, as he trailed up the frozen wooden sidewalk toward the town, he kept looking up at the stars, which were unusually bright, as they always seem over a stretch of snow. He was wondering if there were angels up there, watching the world on Christmas Eve. They came before, on the first Christmas Eve, he knew. Perhaps they kept the Anniversary. He thought about a beautiful coloured picture tacked up in Lesley's bedroom; two angels with white robes and long white wings, flying toward a low hill in the early dawn before sunrise, and on that distant hill, against the soft daybreak light, were three tiny crosses. He never doubted angels looked like that. He was credulous and truthful by nature. There was that look in his blue eyes. He would get it knocked out of him, his mother knew. But she believed he would always keep some of it— enough to make him open-handed and open-hearted.

Tonight Hector had his leather satchel full of Christmas telegrams. After he had delivered them all, he would buy his presents for his mother and the children. The stores sold off their special Christmas things at a discount after eleven o'clock on Christmas Eve.

SIX / Miss Knightly was in Lincoln, attending a convention of Superintendents of Public Instruction, when the long-to-be-remembered blizzard swept down over the prairie State. Travel and telephone service were discontinued. A Chicago passenger train was stalled for three days in a deep cut west of W—. There she lay, and the dining-car had much ado to feed the passengers.

Miss Knightly was snowbound in Lincoln. She tarried there after the convention was dismissed and her fellow superintendents had gone home to their respective counties. She was caught by the storm because she had stayed over to see Julia Marlowe (then young and so fair!) in *The Love Chase*. She was not inconsolable to be delayed for some days. Why worry? She was staying at a small but very pleasant hotel, where the food was good and the beds were comfortable. She was New England born and bred, too conscientious to stay over in the city from mere self-indulgence, but quite willing to be lost to MacAlpin and X— County by the intervention of fate. She stayed, in fact, a week, greatly enjoying such luxuries as plenty of running water, hot baths, and steam heat. At that date MacAlpin houses, and even her office in the Court House, were heated by hard-coal stoves.

At last she was jogging home on a passenger train which left Lincoln at a convenient hour (it was two hours late, travel was still disorganized), when she was pleased to see Mr. Redman in conductor's uniform come into the car. Two of his boys had been her pupils when she taught in high school, before she was elected to a county office. Mr. Redman also seemed pleased, and after he had been through the train to punch tickets, he came back and sat down in the green plush seat opposite Miss Knightly and began to "tease."

"I hear there was a story going up at the Court House that you'd eloped. I was hoping you hadn't made a mistake."

"No. I thought it over and avoided the mistake. But what about you, Mr. Redman? You belong on the run west out of MacAlpin, don't you?"

"I don't know where I belong, Ma'm, and nobody else does. This is Jack Kelly's run, but he got his leg broke trying to help the train crew shovel the sleeping-car loose in that deep cut out of W—. The passengers were just freezing. This blizzard has upset everything. There's got to be better organization from higher up. This has taught us we just can't handle an emergency. Hard on stock, hard on people. A little neighbour of ours—why, you must know her, she was one of your teachers—Jim Ferguesson's little girl. She got pneumonia out there in the country and died out there."

Miss Knightly went so white that Redman without a word hurried to the end of the car and brought back a glass of water. He kept muttering that he was sorry . . . that he "always put his foot in it."

She did not disappoint him. She came back quickly. "That's all right, Mr. Redman. I'd rather hear it before I get home. Did she get lost in the storm? I don't understand."

Mr. Redman sat down and did the best he could to repair damages.

"No, Ma'm, little Lesley acted very sensible, didn't lose her head. You see, the storm struck us about three o'clock in the afternoon. The whole day it had been mild and soft, like spring. Then it came down instanter, like a thousand tons of snow dumped out of the sky. My wife was out in the back yard taking in some clothes she'd hung to dry. She hadn't even a shawl over her head. The suddenness of it confused her so (she couldn't see three feet before her), she wandered around in our back yard, couldn't find her way back to the house. Pretty soon our old dog—he's part shepherd—came yappin' and whinin'. She dropped the clothes and held onto his hair, and he got her to the back porch. That's how bad it was in MacAlpin."

"And Lesley?" Miss Knightly murmured.

"Yes, Ma'm! I'm coming to that. Her scholars tell about how the schoolroom got a little dark, and they all looked out, and there was no graveyard, and no horses that some of them had rode to school on. The boys jumped up to run out and see after the horses, but Lesley stood with her back against the door and wouldn't let 'em go out. Told 'em it would be over in a few minutes. Well, you see it wasn't. Over four feet of snow fell in less'n an hour. About six o'clock some of the fathers of the children that lived aways off started out on horseback, but the horses waded belly-deep, and a wind come up and it turned cold.

"Ford Robertson is the nearest neighbour, you know,—scarcely more than across the road—eighth of a mile, maybe. As soon as he come in from his corral—the Herefords had all bunched up together, over a hundred of 'em, under the lee of a big haystack, and he knew they wouldn't freeze. As soon as he got in, the missus made him go over to the schoolhouse an' take a rope along an' herd 'em all over to her house, teacher an' all, with the boys leading their horses. That night Mrs. Robertson cooked nearly everything in the house for their supper, and she sent Ford upstairs to help Lesley make shakedown beds on the floor. Mrs. Robertson remembers when the big supper was ready and the children ate like wolves, Lesley didn't eat much —said she had a little headache. Next morning she was pretty sick. That day all the fathers came on horse-back for the children. Robertson got one of them to go for old Doctor Small, and he came down on his horse. Doctor said it was pneumonia, and there wasn't much he could do. She didn't seem to have strength to rally. She was out of her head when he got there. She was mostly unconscious for three days, and just slipped out. The funeral is tomorrow. The roads are open now. They were to bring her home today."

The train stopped at a station, and Mr. Redman went to attend to his duties. When he next came through the car Miss Knightly spoke to him. She had recovered herself. Her voice was steady, though very low and very soft when she asked him:

"Were any of her family out there with her when she was ill?"

"Why, yes, Mrs. Ferguesson was out there. That boy Hector got his mother through, before the roads were open. He'd stop at a farmhouse and explain the situation and borrow a team and get the farmer or one of his hands to give them a lift to the next farm, and there they'd get a lift a little further. Everybody knew about the school and the teacher by that time, and wanted to help, no matter how bad the roads were. You see, Miss Knightly, everything would have gone better if it hadn't come on so freezing cold, and if the snow hadn't been so darn soft when it first fell. That family are terrible broke up. We all are, down at the depot. She didn't recognize them when they got there, I heard."

SEVEN/ Twenty years after that historic blizzard Evangeline Knightly—now Mrs. Ralph Thorndike—alighted from the fast eastbound passenger at the MacAlpin station. No one at the station knew who she was except the station master, and he was not quite sure. She looked older, but she also looked more prosperous, more worldly. When she approached him at his office door and asked, "Isn't this Mr. Beardsley?" he recognized her voice and speech.

"That's who. And it's my guess this is, or used to be, Miss Knightly. I've been here almost forever. No ambition. But you left us a long time ago. You're looking fine, Ma'm, if I may say so."

She thanked him and asked him to recommend a hotel where she could stay for a day or two.

He scratched his head. "Well, the Plummer House ain't no Waldorf-Astoria, but the travelling men give a good report of it. The Bishop always stays there when he comes to town. You like me to telephone for an otto [automobile] to take you up? Lord, when you left here there wasn't an otto in the town!"

Mrs. Thorndike smiled. "Not many in the world, I think. And can you tell me, Mr. Beardsley, where the Ferguessons live?"

"The depot Ferguessons? Oh, they live uptown now. Ferg built right west of the Court House, right next to where the Donaldsons used to live. You'll find lots of changes. Some's come up, and some's come down. We used to laugh at Ferg and tell him politics didn't bring in the bacon. But he's got it on us now. The Democrats are sure grand job-givers. Throw 'em round for value received. I still vote the Republican ticket. Too old to change. Anyhow, all those new jobs don't affect the railroads much. They can't put a college professor on to run trains. Now I'll telephone for an otto for you."

Miss Knightly, after going to Denver, had married a very successful young architect, from New England, like herself, and now she was on her way back to Brunswick, Maine, to revisit the scenes of her childhood. Although she had never been in MacAlpin since she left it fifteen years ago, she faithfully read the MacAlpin *Messenger* and knew the important changes in the town.

After she had settled her room at the hotel, and unpacked her toilet articles, she took a cardboard box she had brought with her in the sleeping-car, and went out on a personal errand. She came back to the hotel late for lunch—had a tray sent up to her room, and at four o'clock went to the office in the Court House which used to be her office. This was the autumn of the year, and she had a great desire to drive out among the country schools and see how much fifteen years had changed the land, the pupils, the teachers.

When she introduced herself to the present incumbent, she was cordially received. The young Superintendent seemed a wide-awake, breezy girl, with bobbed blond hair and crimson lips. Her name was Wanda Bliss.

Mrs. Thorndike explained that her stay would not be long enough to let her visit all the country schools, but she would like Miss Bliss's advice as to which were the most interesting.

"Oh, I can run you around to nearly all of them in a day, in my car!"

Mrs. Thorndike thanked her warmly. She liked young people who were not in the least afraid of life or luck or responsibility. In her own youth there were very few like that. The teachers, and many of the pupils out in the country schools, were eager—but anxious. She laughed and told Miss Bliss that she meant to hire a buggy, if there was such a thing left in Mac-Alpin, and drive out into the country alone.

"I get you. You want to put on an old-home act. You might phone around to any farmers you used to know. Some of them still keep horses for haying."

Mrs. Thorndike got a list of the country teachers and the districts in which they taught. A few of them had been pupils in the schools she used to visit. Those she was determined to see.

The following morning she made the call she had stopped off at MacAlpin to make. She rang the doorbell at the house pointed out to her, and through the open window heard a voice call: "Come in, come in, please. I can't answer the bell."

Mrs. Thorndike opened the door into a shining oak hall with a shining oak stairway.

"Come right through, please. I'm in the back parlour. I sprained my ankle and can't walk yet."

The visitor followed the voice and found Mrs. Ferguesson sitting in a spring rocker, her bandaged right foot resting on a low stool.

"Come in, Ma'm. I have a bad sprain, and the little girl who does for me is downtown marketing. Maybe you came to see Mr. Ferguesson, but his office is—" here she broke off and looked up sharply—intently—at her guest. When the guest smiled, she broke out: "Miss Knightly! *Are* you Miss Knightly? Can it be?"

"They call me Mrs. Thorndike now, but I'm Evangeline Knightly just the same." She put out her hand, and Mrs. Ferguesson seized it with both her own.

"It's too good to be true!" she gasped with tears in her voice, "just too good to be true. The things we dream about that way don't happen." She held fast to Mrs. Thorndike's hand as if she were afraid she might vanish. "When did you come to town, and why didn't they let me know!"

"I came only yesterday, Mrs. Ferguesson, and I wanted to slip in on you just like this, with no one else around."

"Mr. Ferguesson must have known. But his mind is always off on some trail, and he never brings me any news when I'm laid up like this. Dear me! It's a long time." She pressed the visitor's hand again before she released it. "Get yourself a comfortable chair, dear, and sit down by me. I do hate to be helpless like this. It wouldn't have happened but for those slippery front stairs. Mr. Ferguesson just wouldn't put a carpet on them, because he says folks don't carpet hardwood stairs, and I tried to answer the doorbell in a hurry, and this is what come of it. I'm not naturally a clumsy woman on my feet."

Mrs. Thorndike noticed an aggrieved tone in her talk which had never been there in the old days when she had so much to be aggrieved about. She brought a chair and sat down close to Mrs. Ferguesson, facing her. The good woman had not changed much, she thought. There was a little grey in her crinkly auburn hair, and there were lines about her mouth which used not to be there, but her eyes had all the old fire.

"How comfortably you are fixed here, Mrs. Ferguesson! I'm so glad to find you like this."

"Yes, we're comfortable—now that they're all gone!

It's mostly his taste. He took great interest." She spoke rather absently, and kept looking out through the polished hall toward the front door, as if she were expecting someone. It seemed a shame that anyone naturally so energetic should be enduring this foolish antiquated method of treating a sprain. The chief change in her, Mrs. Thorndike thought, was that she had grown softer. She reached for the visitor's hand again and held it fast. Tears came to her eyes.

Mrs. Thorndike ventured that she had found the town much changed for the better.

Yes, Mrs. Ferguesson supposed it was.

Then Mrs. Thorndike began in earnest. "How wonderful it is that all your sons have turned out so well! I take the MacAlpin paper chiefly to keep track of the Ferguesson boys. You and Mr. Ferguesson must be very proud."

"Yes'm, we are. We are thankful."

"Even the Denver papers have long articles about Hector and Homer and their great sheep ranches in Wyoming. And Vincent has become such a celebrated chemist, and is helping to destroy all the irreducible elements that I learned when I went to school. And Bryan is with Marshall Field!"

Mrs. Ferguesson nodded and pressed her hand, but she still kept looking down the hall toward the front door. Suddenly she turned with all herself to Mrs. Thorndike and with a storm of tears cried out from her heart: "Oh, Miss Knightly, talk to me about my Lesley! Seems so many have forgot her, but I know you haven't."

"No, Mrs. Ferguesson, I never forget her. Yesterday morning I took a box of roses that I brought with me from my own garden down to where she sleeps. I was glad to find a little seat there, so that I could stay for a long while and think about her."

"Oh, I wish I could have gone with you, Miss

Knightly! (I can't call you anything else.) I wish we could have gone together. I can't help feeling she knows. *Anyhow,* we know! And there's nothing in all my life so precious to me to remember and think about as my Lesley. I'm no soft woman, either. The boys will tell you that. They'll tell you they got on because I always had a firm hand over them. They're all true to Lesley, my boys. Every time they come home they go down there. They feel it like I do, as if it had happened yesterday. Their father feels it, too, when he's not taken up with his abstractions. Anyhow, I don't think men feel things like women and boys. My boys have stayed boys. I do believe they feel as bad as I do about moving up here. We have four nice bedrooms upstairs to make them comfortable, should they all come home at once, and they're polite about us and tell us how well fixed we are. But Miss Knightly, I know at the bottom of their hearts they wish they was back in the old house down by the depot, sleeping in the attic."

Mrs. Thorndike stroked her hand. "I looked for the old house as I was coming up from the station. I made the driver stop."

"Ain't it dreadful, what's been done to it? If I'd foreseen, I'd never have let Mr. Ferguesson sell it. It was in my name. I'd have kept it to go back to and remember sometimes. Folks in middle age make a mistake when they think they can better themselves. They can't, not if they have any heart. And the other kind don't matter—they aren't real people—just poor put-ons, that try to be like the advertisements. Father even took me to California one winter. I was miserable all the time. And there were plenty more like me—miserable underneath. The women lined up in cafeterias, carrying their little trays—like convicts, seemed to me—and running to beauty shops to get their poor old hands manicured. And the old men, Miss Knightly, I pitied them most of all! Old bent-backed farmers, standing round in their shirt-sleeves, in plazas and alleyways, pitching horseshoes like they used to do at home. I tell you, people are happiest where they've had their children and struggled along and been real folks, and not tourists. What do you think about all this running around, Miss Knightly? You're an educated woman, I never had much schooling."

"I don't think schooling gives people any wisdom, Mrs. Ferguesson. I guess only life does that."

"Well, this I know: our best years are when we're working hardest and going right ahead when we can hardly see our way out. Times I was a good deal perplexed. But I always had one comfort. I did own our own house. I never had to worry about the rent. Don't it seem strange to you, though, that all our boys are so practical, and their father such a dreamer?"

Mrs. Thorndike murmured that some people think boys are most likely to take after their mother.

Mrs. Ferguesson smiled absently and shook her head. Presently she came out with: "It's a comfort to me up here, on a still night I can still hear the trains whistle in. Sometimes, when I can't sleep, I lie and listen for them. And I can almost think I am down there, with my children up in the loft. We were very happy." She looked up at her guest and smiled bravely. "I suppose you go away tonight?"

Mrs. Thorndike explained her plan to spend a day in the country.

"You're going out to visit the little schools? Why, God bless you, dear! You're still our Miss Knightly! But you'd better take a car, so you can get up to the Wild Rose school and back in one day. Do go there! The teacher is Mandy Perkins—she was one of her little scholars. You'll like Mandy, an' she loved Lesley. You must get Bud Sullivan to drive you. Engage him right now—the telephone's there in the hall, and the garage is 306. He'll creep along for you, if you tell him. He does for me. I often go out to the Wild Rose school, and over to see dear Mrs. Robertson, who ain't so young as she was then. I can't go with Mr. Ferguesson. He drives so fast it's no satisfaction. And then he's not always mindful. He's had some accidents. When he gets to thinking, he's just as likely to run down a cow as not. He's had to pay for one. You know cows will cross the road right in front of a car. Maybe their grandchildren calves will be more modern-minded."

Mrs. Thorndike did not see her old friend again, but she wrote her a long letter from Wiscasset, Maine, which Mrs. Ferguesson sent to her son Hector, marked, "To be returned, but first pass on to your brothers."

Paul's Case*

IT WAS Paul's afternoon to appear before the faculty of the Pittsburgh High School to account for his various misdemeanours. He had been suspended a week ago, and his father had called at the Principal's office and confessed his perplexity about his son. Paul entered the faculty room suave and smiling. His clothes were a trifle outgrown, and the tan velvet on the collar of his open overcoat was frayed and worn; but for all that there was something of the dandy about him, and he wore an opal pin in his neatly knotted black four-in-hand, and a red carnation in his buttonhole. This latter adornment the faculty somehow felt was not properly significant of the contrite spirit befitting a boy under the ban of suspension.

Paul was tall for his age and very thin, with high, cramped shoulders and a narrow chest. His eyes were remarkable for a certain hysterical brilliancy, and he continually used them in a conscious, theatrical sort of

* From *The Troll Garden*, 1905, and *Youth and the Bright Medusa*, 1920.

way, peculiarly offensive in a boy. The pupils were abnormally large, as though he were addicted to belladonna, but there was a glassy glitter about them which that drug does not produce.

When questioned by the Principal as to why he was there, Paul stated, politely enough, that he wanted to come back to school. This was a lie, but Paul was quite accustomed to lying; found it, indeed, indispensable for overcoming friction. His teachers were asked to state their respective charges against him, which they did with such a rancour and aggrievedness as evinced that this was not a usual case. Disorder and impertinence were among the offences named, yet each of his instructors felt that it was scarcely possible to put into words the real cause of the trouble, which lay in a sort of hysterically defiant manner of the boy's; in the contempt which they all knew he felt for them, and which he seemingly made not the least effort to conceal. Once, when he had been making a synopsis of a paragraph at the blackboard, his English teacher had stepped to his side and attempted to guide his hand. Paul had started back with a shudder and thrust his hands violently behind him. The astonished woman could scarcely have been more hurt and embarrassed had he struck at her. The insult was so involuntary and definitely personal as to be unforgettable. In one way and another, he had made all his teachers, men and women alike, conscious of the same feeling of physical aversion. In one class he habitually sat with his hand shading his eyes; in another he always looked out of the window during the recitation; in another he made a running commentary on the lecture, with humorous intent.

His teachers felt this afternoon that his whole attitude was symbolized by his shrug and his flippantly red carnation flower, and they fell upon him without mercy, his English teacher leading the pack. He stood through it smiling, his pale lips parted over his white teeth. (His lips were continually twitching, and he had a habit of raising his eyebrows that was contemptuous and irritating to the last degree.) Older boys than Paul had broken down and shed tears under that ordeal, but his set smile did not once desert him, and his only sign of discomfort was the nervous trembling of the fingers that toyed with the buttons of his overcoat, and an occasional jerking of the other hand which held his hat. Paul was always smiling, always glancing about him, seeming to feel that people might be watching him and trying to detect something. This conscious expression, since it was as far as possible from boyish mirthfulness, was usually attributed to insolence or "smartness."

As the inquisition proceeded, one of his instructors repeated an impertinent remark of the boy's, and the Principal asked him whether he thought that a courteous speech to make to a woman. Paul shrugged his shoulders slightly and his eyebrows twitched.

"I don't know," he replied. "I didn't mean to be polite or impolite, either. I guess it's a sort of way I have, of saying things regardless."

The Principal asked him whether he didn't think that a way it would be well to get rid of. Paul grinned and said he guessed so. When he was told that he could go, he bowed gracefully and went out. His bow was like a repetition of the scandalous red carnation.

His teachers were in despair, and his drawing master voiced the feeling of them all when he declared there was something about the boy which none of them understood. He added: "I don't really believe that smile of his comes altogether from insolence; there's something sort of haunted about it. The boy is not strong, for one thing. There is something wrong about the fellow."

The drawing master had come to realize that, in

looking at Paul, one saw only his white teeth and the forced animation of his eyes. One warm afternoon the boy had gone to sleep at his drawing-board, and his master had noted with amazement what a white, blue-veined face it was; drawn and wrinkled like an old man's about the eyes, the lips twitching even in his sleep.

His teachers left the building dissatisfied and unhappy; humiliated to have felt so vindictive toward a mere boy, to have uttered this feeling in cutting terms, and to have set each other on, as it were, in the grewsome game of intemperate reproach. One of them remembered having seen a miserable street cat set at bay by a ring of tormentors.

As for Paul, he ran down the hill whistling the Soldiers' Chorus from *Faust*, looking wildly behind him now and then to see whether some of his teachers were not there to witness his light-heartedness. As it was now late in the afternoon and Paul was on duty that evening as usher at Carnegie Hall, he decided that he would not go home to supper.

When he reached the concert hall the doors were not yet open. It was chilly outside, and he decided to go up into the picture gallery—always deserted at this hour—where there were some of Raffelli's gay studies of Paris streets and an airy blue Venetian scene or two that always exhilarated him. He was delighted to find no one in the gallery but the old guard, who sat in the corner, a newspaper on his knee, a black patch over one eye and the other closed. Paul possessed himself of the place and walked confidently up and down, whistling under his breath. After a while he sat down before a blue Rico and lost himself. When he bethought him to look at his watch, it was after seven o'clock, and he rose with a start and ran downstairs, making a face at Augustus Cæsar, peering out from the cast-room, and an evil gesture at the Venus of Milo as he passed her on the stairway.

When Paul reached the ushers' dressing-room half-a-dozen boys were there already, and he began excitedly to tumble into his uniform. It was one of the few that at all approached fitting, and Paul thought it very becoming—though he knew the tight, straight coat accentuated his narrow chest, about which he was exceedingly sensitive. He was always excited while he dressed, twanging all over to the tuning of the strings and the preliminary flourishes of the horns in the music-room; but tonight he seemed quite beside himself, and he teased and plagued the boys until, telling him that he was crazy, they put him down on the floor and sat on him.

Somewhat calmed by his suppression, Paul dashed out to the front of the house to seat the early comers. He was a model usher. Gracious and smiling he ran up and down the aisles. Nothing was too much trouble for him; he carried messages and brought programs as though it were his greatest pleasure in life, and all the people in his section thought him a charming boy, feeling that he remembered and admired them. As the house filled, he grew more and more vivacious and animated, and the colour came to his cheeks and lips. It was very much as though this were a great reception and Paul were the host. Just as the musicians came out to take their places, his English teacher arrived with checks for the seats which a prominent manufacturer had taken for the season. She betrayed some embarrassment when she handed Paul the tickets, and a *hauteur* which subsequently made her feel very foolish. Paul was startled for a moment, and had the feeling of wanting to put her out; what business had she here among all these fine people and gay colours? He looked her over and decided that she was not appropriately dressed and must be a fool to sit downstairs in such togs. The tickets had probably been sent her out of kindness, he reflected, as he put down a seat for her, and she had about as much right to sit there as he had.

When the symphony began Paul sank into one of the rear seats with a long sigh of relief, and lost himself as he had done before the Rico. It was not that symphonies, as such, meant anything in particular to Paul, but the first sigh of the instruments seemed to free some hilarious spirit within him; something that struggled there like the Genius in the bottle found by the Arab fisherman. He felt a sudden zest of life; the lights danced before his eyes and the concert hall blazed into unimaginable splendour. When the soprano soloist came on, Paul forgot even the nastiness of his teacher's being there, and gave himself up to the peculiar intoxication such personages always had for him. The soloist chanced to be a German woman, by no means in her first youth, and the mother of many children; but she wore a satin gown and a tiara, and she had that indefinable air of achievement, that world-shine upon her, which always blinded Paul to any possible defects.

After a concert was over, Paul was often irritable and wretched until he got to sleep,—and tonight he was even more than usually restless. He had the feeling of not being able to let down; of its being impossible to give up this delicious excitement which was the only thing that could be called living at all. During the last number he withdrew and, after hastily changing his clothes in the dressing-room, slipped out to the side door where the singer's carriage stood. Here he began pacing rapidly up and down the walk, waiting to see her come out.

Over yonder the Schenley, in its vacant stretch,

loomed big and square through the fine rain, the windows of its twelve stories glowing like those of a
lighted card-board house under a Christmas tree. All
the actors and singers of any importance stayed there
when they were in the city, and a number of the big
manufacturers of the place lived there in the winter.
Paul had often hung about the hotel, watching the
people go in and out, longing to enter and leave
school-masters and dull care behind him for ever.

At last the singer came out, accompanied by the
conductor, who helped her into her carriage and
closed the door with a cordial *auf wiedersehen*,—
which set Paul to wondering whether she were not an
old sweetheart of his. Paul followed the carriage over
to the hotel, walking so rapidly as not to be far from
the entrance when the singer alighted and disappeared behind the swinging glass doors which were
opened by a negro in a tall hat and a long coat. In
the moment that the door was ajar, it seemed to Paul
that he, too, entered. He seemed to feel himself go
after her up the steps, into the warm, lighted building,
into an exotic, a tropical world of shiny, glistening sur-
faces and basking ease. He reflected upon the mysterious dishes that were brought into the dining-room,
the green bottles in buckets of ice, as he had seen
them in the supper party pictures of the Sunday supplement. A quick gust of wind brought the rain down
with sudden vehemence, and Paul was startled to find
that he was still outside in the slush of the gravel
driveway; that his boots were letting in the water and
his scanty overcoat was clinging wet about him; that
the lights in front of the concert hall were out, and
that the rain was driving in sheets between him and
the orange glow of the windows above him. There it
was, what he wanted—tangibly before him, like the
fairy world of a Christmas pantomime; as the rain beat

in his face, Paul wondered whether he were destined always to shiver in the black night outside, looking up at it.

He turned and walked reluctantly toward the car tracks. The end had to come sometime; his father in his night-clothes at the top of the stairs, explanations that did not explain, hastily improvised fictions that were forever tripping him up, his upstairs room and its horrible yellow wall-paper, the creaking bureau with the greasy plush collar-box, and over his painted wooden bed the pictures of George Washington and John Calvin, and the framed motto, "Feed my Lambs," which had been worked in red worsted by his mother, whom Paul could not remember.

Half an hour later, Paul alighted from the Negley Avenue car and went slowly down one of the side streets off the main thoroughfare. It was a highly respectable street, where all the houses were exactly alike, and where business men of moderate means begot and reared large families of children, all of whom went to Sabbath-school and learned the shorter catechism, and were interested in arithmetic; all of whom were as exactly alike as their homes, and of a piece with the monotony in which they lived. Paul never went up Cordelia Street without a shudder of loathing. His home was next the house of the Cumberland minister. He approached it tonight with the nerveless sense of defeat, the hopeless feeling of sinking back forever into ugliness and commonness that he had always had when he came home. The moment he turned into Cordelia Street he felt the waters close above his head. After each of these orgies of living, he experienced all the physical depression which follows a debauch; the loathing of respectable beds, of common food, of a house permeated by kitchen odours; a shuddering repulsion for the flavourless, colourless mass of every-day existence; a morbid desire for cool things and soft lights and fresh flowers.

The nearer he approached the house, the more absolutely unequal Paul felt to the sight of it all; his ugly sleeping chamber; the cold bath-room with the grimy zinc tub, the cracked mirror, the dripping spiggots; his father, at the top of the stairs, his hairy legs sticking out from his nightshirt, his feet thrust into carpet slippers. He was so much later than usual that there would certainly be inquiries and reproaches. Paul stopped short before the door. He felt that he could not be accosted by his father tonight; that he could not toss again on that miserable bed. He would not go in. He would tell his father that he had no car fare, and it was raining so hard he had gone home with one of the boys and stayed all night.

Meanwhile, he was wet and cold. He went around to the back of the house and tried one of the basement windows, found it open, raised it cautiously, and scrambled down the cellar wall to the floor. There he stood, holding his breath, terrified by the noise he had made; but the floor above him was silent, and there was no creak on the stairs. He found a soap-box, and carried it over to the soft ring of light that streamed from the furnace door, and sat down. He was horribly afraid of rats, so he did not try to sleep, but sat looking distrustfully at the dark, still terrified lest he might have awakened his father. In such reactions, after one of the experiences which made days and nights out of the dreary blanks of the calendar, when his senses were deadened, Paul's head was always singularly clear. Suppose his father had heard him getting in at the window and had come down and shot him for a burglar? Then, again, suppose his father had come down, pistol in hand, and he had cried out in time to save himself, and his father had been horrified to think how nearly he had killed him? Then, again, suppose a day should come when his father would remember that night, and wish there had been no warning cry to stay his hand? With this last supposition Paul entertained himself until daybreak.

The following Sunday was fine; the sodden November chill was broken by the last flash of autumnal summer. In the morning Paul had to go to church and Sabbath-school, as always. On seasonable Sunday afternoons the burghers of Cordelia Street usually sat out on their front "stoops," and talked to their neighbours on the next stoop, or called to those across the street in neighbourly fashion. The men sat placidly on gay cushions placed upon the steps that led down to the sidewalk, while the women, in their Sunday "waists," sat in rockers on the cramped porches, pretending to be greatly at their ease. The children played in the streets; there were so many of them that the place resembled the recreation grounds of a kindergarten. The men on the steps—all in their shirt sleeves, their vests unbuttoned—sat with their legs well apart, their stomachs comfortably protruding, and talked of the prices of things, or told anecdotes of the sagacity of their various chiefs and overlords. They occasionally looked over the multitude of squabbling children, listened affectionately to their high-pitched, nasal voices, smiling to see their own proclivities reproduced in their offspring, and interspersed their legends of the iron kings with remarks about their sons' progress at school, their grades in arithmetic, and the amounts they had saved in their toy banks.

On this last Sunday of November, Paul sat all the afternoon on the lowest step of his "stoop," staring into the street, while his sisters, in their rockers, were talking to the minister's daughters next door about how many shirt-waists they had made in the last week, and how many waffles some one had eaten at the last

church supper. When the weather was warm, and his
father was in a particularly jovial frame of mind, the
girls made lemonade, which was always brought out
in a red-glass pitcher, ornamented with forget-me-nots
in blue enamel. This the girls thought very fine, and
the neighbours joked about the suspicious colour of
the pitcher.

Today Paul's father, on the top step, was talking to
a young man who shifted a restless baby from knee to
knee. He happened to be the young man who was
daily held up to Paul as a model, and after whom it
was his father's dearest hope that he would pattern.
This young man was of a ruddy complexion, with a
compressed, red mouth, and faded, near-sighted eyes,
over which he wore thick spectacles, with gold bows
that curved about his ears. He was clerk to one of the
magnates of a great steel corporation, and was looked
upon in Cordelia Street as a young man with a future.
There was a story that, some five years ago—he was
now barely twenty-six—he had been a trifle "dis-
sipated," but in order to curb his appetites and save
the loss of time and strength that a sowing of wild
oats might have entailed, he had taken his chief's
advice, oft reiterated to his employés, and at twenty-
one had married the first woman whom he could persuade to share his fortunes. She happened to be an
angular school-mistress, much older than he, who also
wore thick glasses, and who had now borne him four
children, all near-sighted, like herself.

The young man was relating how his chief, now
cruising in the Mediterranean, kept in touch with all
the details of the business, arranging his office hours
on his yacht just as though he were at home, and
"knocking off work enough to keep two stenographers
busy." His father told, in turn, the plan his corporation was considering, of putting in an electric railway
plant at Cairo. Paul snapped his teeth; he had an awful

apprehension that they might spoil it all before he got there. Yet he rather liked to hear these legends of the iron kings, that were told and retold on Sundays and holidays; these stories of palaces in Venice, yachts on the Mediterranean, and high play at Monte Carlo appealed to his fancy, and he was interested in the triumphs of cash boys who had become famous, though he had no mind for the cash-boy stage.

After supper was over, and he had helped to dry the dishes, Paul nervously asked his father whether he could go to George's to get some help in his geometry, and still more nervously asked for car-fare. This latter request he had to repeat, as his father, on principle, did not like to hear requests for money, whether much or little. He asked Paul whether he could not go to some boy who lived nearer, and told him that he ought not to leave his school work until Sunday; but he gave him the dime. He was not a poor man, but he had a worthy ambition to come up in the world. His only reason for allowing Paul to usher was that he thought a boy ought to be earning a little.

Paul bounded upstairs, scrubbed the greasy odour of the dish-water from his hands with the ill-smelling soap he hated, and then shook over his fingers a few drops of violet water from the bottle he kept hidden in his drawer. He left the house with his geometry conspicuously under his arm, and the moment he got out of Cordelia Street and boarded a downtown car, he shook off the lethargy of two deadening days, and began to live again.

The leading juvenile of the permanent stock company which played at one of the downtown theatres was an acquaintance of Paul's, and the boy had been invited to drop in at the Sunday-night rehearsals whenever he could. For more than a year Paul had spent every available moment loitering about Charley Edwards's dressing-room. He had won a place among

Edwards's following not only because the young actor, who could not afford to employ a dresser, often found him useful, but because he recognized in Paul something akin to what churchmen term "vocation."

It was at the theatre and at Carnegie Hall that Paul really lived; the rest was but a sleep and a forgetting. This was Paul's fairy tale, and it had for him all the allurement of a secret love. The moment he inhaled the gassy, painty, dusty odour behind the scenes, he breathed like a prisoner set free, and felt within him the possibility or doing or saying splendid, brilliant things. The moment the cracked orchestra beat out the overture from *Martha*, or jerked at the serenade from *Rigoletto*, all stupid and ugly things slid from him, and his senses were deliciously, yet delicately fired.

Perhaps it was because, in Paul's world, the natural nearly always wore the guise of ugliness, that a certain element of artificiality seemed to him necessary in beauty. Perhaps it was because his experience of life elsewhere was so full of Sabbath-school picnics, petty economies, wholesome advice as to how to succeed in life, and the unescapable odours of cooking, that he found this existence so alluring, these smartly-clad men and women so attractive, that he was so moved by these starry apple orchards that bloomed perennially under the lime-light.

It would be difficult to put it strongly enough how convincingly the stage entrance of that theatre was for Paul the actual portal of Romance. Certainly none of the company ever suspected it, least of all Charley Edwards. It was very like the old stories that used to float about London of fabulously rich Jews, who had subterranean halls, with palms, and fountains, and soft lamps, and richly apparelled women who never saw the disenchanting light of London day. So, in the midst of that smoke-palled city, enamoured of figures and grimy toil, Paul had his secret temple, his wishing-carpet, his bit of blue-and-white Mediterranean shore bathed in perpetual sunshine.

Several of Paul's teachers had a theory that his imagination had been perverted by garish fiction; but the truth was, he scarcely ever read at all. The books at home were not such as would either tempt or corrupt a youthful mind, and as for reading the novels that some of his friends urged upon him—well, he got what he wanted much more quickly from music; any sort of music, from an orchestra to a barrel organ. He needed only the spark, the indescribable thrill that made his imagination master of his senses, and he could make plots and pictures enough of his own. It was equally true that he was not stage-struck—not, at any rate, in the usual acceptation of that expression. He had no desire to become an actor, any more than he had to become a musician. He felt no necessity to do any of these things; what he wanted was to see, to be in the atmosphere, float on the wave of it, to be carried out, blue league after blue league, away from everything.

After a night behind the scenes, Paul found the schoolroom more than ever repulsive; the bare floors and naked walls; the prosy men who never wore frock coats, or violets in their buttonholes; the women with their dull gowns, shrill voices, and pitiful seriousness about prepositions that govern the dative. He could not bear to have the other pupils think, for a moment, that he took these people seriously; he must convey to them that he considered it all trivial, and was there only by way of a joke, anyway. He had autograph pictures of all the members of the stock company which he showed his classmates, telling them the most incredible stories of his familiarity with these people, of his acquaintance with the soloists who came to Carnegie Hall, his suppers with them and the flowers he sent them. When these stories lost their effect, and his audience grew listless, he would bid all the boys good-bye, announcing that he was going to travel for awhile; going to Naples, to California, to Egypt. Then, next Monday, he would slip back, conscious and nervously smiling; his sister was ill, and he would have to defer his voyage until spring.

Matters went steadily worse with Paul at school. In the itch to let his instructors know how heartily he despised them, and how thoroughly he was appreciated elsewhere, he mentioned once or twice that he had no time to fool with theorems; adding—with a twitch of the eyebrows and a touch of that nervous bravado which so perplexed them—that he was helping the people down at the stock company; they were old friends of his.

The upshot of the matter was, that the Principal went to Paul's father, and Paul was taken out of school and put to work. The manager at Carnegie Hall was told to get another usher in his stead; the door-keeper at the theatre was warned not to admit him to the house; and Charley Edwards remorsefully promised the boy's father not to see him again.

The members of the stock company were vastly amused when some of Paul's stories reached them— especially the women. They were hard-working women, most of them supporting indolent husbands or brothers, and they laughed rather bitterly at having stirred the boy to such fervid and florid inventions. They agreed with the faculty and with his father, that Paul's was a bad case.

The east-bound train was ploughing through a January snow-storm; the dull dawn was beginning to show grey when the engine whistled a mile out of Newark. Paul started up from the seat where he had lain curled in uneasy slumber, rubbed the breath-misted window glass with his hand, and peered out. The snow was whirling in curling eddies above the white bottom lands, and the drifts lay already deep in the fields and along the fences, while here and there the long dead grass and dried weed stalks protruded black above it. Lights shone from the scattered houses, and a gang of labourers who stood beside the track waved their lanterns.

Paul had slept very little, and he felt grimy and un-comfortable. He had made the all-night journey in a day coach because he was afraid if he took a Pullman he might be seen by some Pittsburgh business man who had noticed him in Denny & Carson's office. When the whistle woke him, he clutched quickly at his breast pocket, glancing about him with an un-certain smile. But the little, clay-bespattered Italians were still sleeping, the slatternly women across the aisle were in open-mouthed oblivion, and even the crumby, crying babies were for the nonce stilled. Paul settled back to struggle with his impatience as best he could.

When he arrived at the Jersey City station, he hurried through his breakfast, manifestly ill at ease and keeping a sharp eye about him. After he reached the Twenty-third Street station, he consulted a cab-man, and had himself driven to a men's furnishing establishment which was just opening for the day. He spent upward of two hours there, buying with endless reconsidering and great care. His new street suit he put on in the fitting-room; the frock coat and dress clothes he had bundled into the cab with his new shirts. Then he drove to a hatter's and a shoe house. His next errand was at Tiffany's, where he selected silver mounted brushes and a scarf-pin. He would not wait to have his silver marked, he said.

Lastly, he stopped at a trunk shop on Broadway, and had his purchases packed into various travelling bags.

It was a little after one o'clock when he drove up to the Waldorf, and, after settling with the cabman, went into the office. He registered from Washington; said his mother and father had been abroad, and that he had come down to await the arrival of their steamer. He told his story plausibly and had no trouble, since he offered to pay for them in advance, in engaging his rooms; a sleeping-room, sitting-room and bath.

Not once, but a hundred times Paul had planned this entry into New York. He had gone over every detail of it with Charley Edwards, and in his scrap book at home there were pages of description about New York hotels, cut from the Sunday papers.

When he was shown to his sitting-room on the eighth floor, he saw at a glance that everything was as it should be; there was but one detail in his mental picture that the place did not realize, so he rang for the bell boy and sent him down for flowers. He moved about nervously until the boy returned, putting away his new linen and fingering it delightedly as he did so. When the flowers came, he put them hastily into water, and then tumbled into a hot bath. Presently he came out of his white bath-room, resplendent in his new silk underwear, and playing with the tassels of his red robe. The snow was whirling so fiercely outside his windows that he could scarcely see across the street; but within, the air was deliciously soft and fragrant. He put the violets and jonquils on the tabouret beside the couch, and threw himself down with a long sigh, covering himself with a Roman blanket. He was thoroughly tired; he had been in such haste, he had stood up to such a strain, covered so much ground in the last twenty-four hours, that he wanted to think how it had all come about. Lulled by the sound of the wind, the warm air, and the cool fragrance of the flowers, he sank into deep, drowsy retrospection.

It had been wonderfully simple; when they had shut him out of the theatre and concert hall, when they had taken away his bone, the whole thing was virtually determined. The rest was a mere matter of opportunity. The only thing that at all surprised him was his own courage—for he realized well enough that he had always been tormented by fear, a sort of apprehensive dread that, of late years, as the meshes of the lies he had told closed about him, had been pulling the muscles of his body tighter and tighter. Until now, he could not remember a time when he had not been dreading something. Even when he was a little boy, it was always there—behind him, or before, or on either side. There had always been the shadowed corner, the dark place into which he dared not look, but from which something seemed always to be watching him—and Paul had done things that were not pretty to watch, he knew.

But now he had a curious sense of relief, as though he had at last thrown down the gauntlet to the thing in the corner.

Yet it was but a day since he had been sulking in the traces; but yesterday afternoon that he had been sent to the bank with Denny & Carson's deposit, as usual—but this time he was instructed to leave the book to be balanced. There was above two thousand dollars in checks, and nearly a thousand in the bank notes which he had taken from the book and quietly transferred to his pocket. At the bank he had made out a new deposit slip. His nerves had been steady enough to permit of his returning to the office, where he had finished his work and asked for a full day's holiday tomorrow, Saturday, giving a perfectly reasonable pretext. The bank book, he knew, would not be returned before Monday or Tuesday, and his father would be out of town for the next week. From the time he slipped the bank notes into his pocket until he boarded the night train for New York, he had not known a moment's hesitation.

How astonishingly easy it had all been; here he was, the thing done; and this time there would be no awakening, no figure at the top of the stairs. He watched the snow flakes whirling by his window until he fell asleep.

When he awoke, it was four o'clock in the afternoon. He bounded up with a start; one of his precious days gone already! He spent nearly an hour in dressing, watching every stage of his toilet carefully in the mirror. Everything was quite perfect; he was exactly the kind of boy he had always wanted to be.

When he went downstairs, Paul took a carriage and drove up Fifth avenue toward the Park. The snow had somewhat abated; carriages and tradesmen's wagons were hurrying soundlessly to and fro in the winter twilight; boys in woollen mufflers were shovelling off the doorsteps; the avenue stages made fine spots of colour against the white street. Here and there on the corners whole flower gardens blooming behind glass windows, against which the snow flakes stuck and melted; violets, roses, carnations, lilies of the valley—somehow vastly more lovely and alluring that they blossomed thus unnaturally in the snow. The Park itself was a wonderful stage winter-piece.

When he returned, the pause of the twilight had ceased, and the tune of the streets had changed. The snow was falling faster, lights streamed from the hotels that reared their many stories fearlessly up into the storm, defying the raging Atlantic winds. A long, black stream of carriages poured down the avenue, intersected here and there by other streams, tending horizontally. There were a score of cabs about the entrance of this hotel, and his driver had to wait. Boys in livery were running in and out of the awning stretched across the sidewalk, up and down the red velvet carpet laid from the door to the street. Above, about, within it all, was the rumble and roar, the hurry and toss of thousands of human beings as hot for pleasure as himself, and on every side of him towered the glaring affirmation of the omnipotence of wealth.

The boy set his teeth and drew his shoulders together in a spasm of realization; the plot of all dramas, the text of all romances, the nerve-stuff of all sensations was whirling about him like the snow flakes. He burnt like a faggot in a tempest.

When Paul came down to dinner, the music of the orchestra floated up the elevator shaft to greet him. As he stepped into the thronged corridor, he sank back into one of the chairs against the wall to get his breath. The lights, the chatter, the perfumes, the bewildering medley of colour—he had, for a moment, the feeling of not being able to stand it. But only for a moment; these were his own people, he told himself. He went slowly about the corridors, through the writing-rooms, smoking-rooms, reception-rooms, as though he were exploring the chambers of an enchanted palace, built and peopled for him alone.

When he reached the dining-room he sat down at a table near a window. The flowers, the white linen, the many-coloured wine glasses, the gay toilettes of the women, the low popping of corks, the undulating repetitions of the *Blue Danube* from the orchestra, all flooded Paul's dream with bewildering radiance. When the roseate tinge of his champagne was added—that cold, precious, bubbling stuff that creamed and foamed in his glass—Paul wondered that there were honest men in the world at all. This was what all the world was fighting for, he reflected; this was what all the struggle was about. He doubted the reality of his past. Had he ever known a place called Cordelia Street, a place where fagged looking business men boarded the early car? Mere rivets in a machine they seemed to Paul,—sickening men, with combings of children's hair always hanging to their coats, and the smell of cooking in their clothes. Cordelia Street— Ah, that belonged to another time and country! Had he not always been thus, had he not sat here night after night, from as far back as he could remember, looking pensively over just such shimmering textures, and slowly twirling the stem of a glass like this one between his thumb and middle finger? He rather thought he had.

He was not in the least abashed or lonely. He had no especial desire to meet or to know any of these people; all he demanded was the right to look on and conjecture, to watch the pageant. The mere stage properties were all he contended for. Nor was he lonely later in the evening, in his loge at the Opera. He was entirely rid of his nervous misgivings, of his forced aggressiveness, of the imperative desire to show himself different from his surroundings. He felt now that his surroundings explained him. Nobody questioned the purple; he had only to wear it passively. He had only to glance down at his dress coat to reassure himself that here it would be impossible for anyone to humiliate him.

He found it hard to leave his beautiful sitting-room to go to bed that night, and sat long watching the raging storm from his turret window. When he went to sleep, it was with the lights turned on in his bed-room; partly because of his old timidity, and partly so that, if he should wake in the night, there would be no wretched moment of doubt, no horrible suspicion of yellow wall-paper, or of Washington and Calvin above his bed.

On Sunday morning the city was practically snow-bound. Paul breakfasted late, and in the afternoon he fell in with a wild San Francisco boy, a freshman at Yale, who said he had run down for a "little flyer" over Sunday. The young man offered to show Paul the night side of the town, and the two boys went off together after dinner, not returning to the hotel until seven o'clock the next morning. They had started out in the confiding warmth of a champagne friendship, but their parting in the elevator was singularly cool. The freshman pulled himself together to make his train, and Paul went to bed. He awoke at two o'clock in the afternoon, very thirsty and dizzy, and rang for ice-water, coffee, and the Pittsburgh papers.

On the part of the hotel management, Paul excited no suspicion. There was this to be said for him, that he wore his spoils with dignity and in no way made himself conspicuous. His chief greediness lay in his ears and eyes, and his excesses were not offensive ones. His dearest pleasures were the grey winter twilights in his sitting-room; his quiet enjoyment of his flowers, his clothes, his wide divan, his cigarette and his sense of power. He could not remember a time when he had felt so at peace with himself. The mere release from the necessity of petty lying, lying every day and every day, restored his self-respect. He had never lied for pleasure, even at school; but to make himself noticed and admired, to assert his difference from other Cordelia Street boys; and he felt a good deal more manly, more honest, even, now that he had no need for boastful pretensions, now that he could, as his actor friends used to say, "dress the part." It was characteristic that remorse did not occur to him. His golden days went by without a shadow, and he made each as perfect as he could.

On the eighth day after his arrival in New York, he found the whole affair exploited in the Pittsburgh papers, exploited with a wealth of detail which indicated that local news of a sensational nature was at a low ebb. The firm of Denny & Carson announced that the boy's father had refunded the full amount of his theft, and that they had no intention of prosecuting. The Cumberland minister had been interviewed, and expressed his hope of yet reclaiming the motherless lad, and Paul's Sabbath-school teacher declared that she would spare no effort to that end. The rumour had reached Pittsburgh that the boy had been seen in a New York hotel, and his father had gone East to find him and bring him home.

Paul had just come in to dress for dinner; he sank into a chair, weak in the knees, and clasped his head in his hands. It was to be worse than jail, even; the tepid waters of Cordelia Street were to close over him finally and forever. The grey monotony stretched before him in hopeless, unrelieved years; Sabbath-school, Young People's Meeting, the yellow-papered room, the damp dish-towels; it all rushed back upon him with sickening vividness. He had the old feeling that the orchestra had suddenly stopped, the sinking sensation that the play was over. The sweat broke out on his face, and he sprang to his feet, looked about him with his white, conscious smile, and winked at himself in the mirror. With something of the childish belief in miracles with which he had so often gone to class, all his lessons unlearned, Paul dressed and dashed whistling down the corridor to the elevator.

He had no sooner entered the dining-room and caught the measure of the music, than his remembrance was lightened by his old elastic power of claiming the moment, mounting with it, and finding it all sufficient. The glare and glitter about him, the mere scenic accessories had again, and for the last time, their old potency. He would show himself that he was game, he would finish the thing splendidly.

He doubted, more than ever, the existence of Cordelia Street, and for the first time he drank his wine recklessly. Was he not, after all, one of these fortunate beings? Was he not still himself, and in his own place? He drummed a nervous accompaniment to the music and looked about him, telling himself over and over that it had paid.

He reflected drowsily, to the swell of the violin and the chill sweetness of his wine, that he might have done it more wisely. He might have caught an outbound steamer and been well out of their clutches before now. But the other side of the world had seemed too far away and too uncertain then; he could not have waited for it; his need had been too sharp. If he had to choose over again, he would do the same thing tomorrow. He looked affectionately about the dining-room, now gilded with a soft mist. Ah, it had paid indeed!

Paul was awakened next morning by a painful throbbing in his head and feet. He had thrown himself across the bed without undressing, and had slept with his shoes on. His limbs and hands were lead heavy, and his tongue and throat were parched. There came upon him one of those fateful attacks of clearheadedness that never occurred except when he was physically exhausted and his nerves hung loose. He lay still and closed his eyes and let the tide of realities wash over him.

His father was in New York; "Stopping at some joint or other," he told himself. The memory of successive summers on the front stoop fell upon him like a weight of black water. He had not a hundred dollars left; and he knew now, more than ever, that money was everything, the wall that stood between all he loathed and all he wanted. The thing was winding itself up; he had thought of that on his first glorious day in New York, and had even provided a way to snap the thread. It lay on his dressing-table now; he had got it out last night when he came blindly up from dinner,—but the shiny metal hurt his eyes, and he disliked the look of it, anyway.

He rose and moved about with a painful effort, succumbing now and again to attacks of nausea. It was the old depression exaggerated; all the world had become Cordelia Street. Yet somehow he was not afraid of anything, was absolutely calm; perhaps because he had looked into the dark corner at last, and knew. It was bad enough, what he saw there; but somehow not so bad as his long fear of it had been. He saw everything clearly now. He had a feeling that he had made the best of it, that he had lived the sort of life he was meant to live, and for half an hour he sat staring at the revolver. But he told himself that was not the way, so he went downstairs and took a cab to the ferry.

When Paul arrived at Newark, he got off the train and took another cab, directing the driver to follow the Pennsylvania tracks out of the town. The snow lay heavy on the roadways and had drifted deep in the open fields. Only here and there the dead grass or dried weed stalks projected, singularly black, above it. Once well into the country, Paul dismissed the carriage and walked, floundering along the tracks, his mind a medley of irrelevant things. He seemed to hold in his brain an actual picture of everything he had seen that morning. He remembered every feature of both his drivers, the toothless old woman from whom he had bought the red flowers in his coat, the agent from whom he had got his ticket, and all of his fellow-passengers on the ferry. His mind, unable to cope with vital matters near at hand, worked feverishly and deftly at sorting and grouping these images. They made for him a part of the ugliness of the world, of the ache in his head, and the bitter burning on his tongue. He stooped and put a handful of snow into his mouth as he walked, but that, too, seemed hot. When he reached a little hillside, where the tracks ran through a cut some twenty feet below him, he stopped and sat down.

The carnations in his coat were drooping with the cold, he noticed; all their red glory over. It occurred to him that all the flowers he had seen in the show windows that first night must have gone the same way, long before this. It was only one splendid breath they had, in spite of their brave mockery at the winter outside the glass. It was a losing game in the end, it seemed, this revolt against the homilies by which the world is run. Paul took one of the blossoms carefully from his coat and scooped a little hole in the snow, where he covered it up. Then he dozed a while, from his weak condition, seeming insensible to the cold.

The sound of an approaching train woke him, and he started to his feet, remembering only his resolution, and afraid lest he should be too late. He stood watching the approaching locomotive, his teeth chattering, his lips drawn away from them in a frightened smile; once or twice he glanced nervously sidewise, as though he were being watched. When the right moment came, he jumped. As he fell, the folly of his haste occurred to him with merciless clearness, the vastness of what he had left undone. There flashed through his brain, clearer than ever before, the blue of Adriatic water, the yellow of Algerian sands.

He felt something strike his chest,—his body was being thrown swiftly through the air, on and on, immeasurably far and fast, while his limbs gently relaxed. Then, because the picture making mechanism was crushed, the disturbing visions flashed into black, and Paul dropped back into the immense design of things.

Willa Cather's
Unfinished Avignon Story

AN ARTICLE BY GEORGE N. KATES

N O T yet enough noticed in the career of a "classic" writer like Willa Cather, whose reputation rests— with justice—on her discovery for American letters of regions like Nebraska, is the increasing and finally dominant pull that Europe exerted upon her. It can be traced from the very beginning of her long career; it impregnates the whole body of her work. When for her, about 1922, in a period of internal strain "the world broke in two," there is no doubt upon which half she took her stand. One of the most interesting results of this development, moreover, came in the very last years of her life, a project never completed: to place the setting of a story straight across the world, quite far into the past—leaving America entirely—in the setting of medieval Avignon.

Very little comment has been made in print about the significance of this radical departure. In her old age had Willa Cather played out her interest in the field where she had conquered her fame? Was she moving, very late, even farther into one to which even in the beginning she had given her loyalty? Many problems are involved, and the situation is complex.

The chief mention of the little that has been published is on page 190 of her friend Edith Lewis's *Willa Cather Living*, a most sensitive book, which happily makes good some of our lacks because of the adamant fate that Willa Cather reserved for those of her letters and papers she did not herself destroy. Miss Lewis has chronicled the chief facts with care:

> She had wanted for years to write an Avignon story. On her many journeys to the south of France, it was Avignon that left the deepest impression with her. The Papal Palace at Avignon —seen first when she was a girl—stirred her as

no building in the world had ever done. In 1935 we were there together. One day, as we wandered through the great chambers of white, almost translucent stone, alone except for a guide, this young fellow suddenly stopped still in one of the rooms and began to sing, with a beautiful voice. It echoed down the corridors and under the arched ceilings like a great bell sounding—but sounding from some remote past; its vibrations seemed laden, weighted down with the passions of another age—cruelties, splendours, lost and unimaginable to us in our time.

I have sometimes thought that Willa Cather wished to make her story like this song.

She had brought with her [on a journey in June 1941, six years before her death] to San Francisco Okey's little history of Avignon; and she often spent her mornings on the open roof garden of the Fairmont, walking to and fro, and reading in this book. It was probably then that she planned the general outline of the Avignon story.

The manuscript, by Willa Cather's direction, was destroyed after her death; and it is a heavy loss. It had been in her mind to succeed *Sapphira and the Slave Girl*, of 1940 (her last published work, except for the stories gathered together under the heading of *The Old Beauty*, which were issued posthumously in 1948); and although these last years became a period of illness and non-productivity, the story's place at the terminus of the great swing of her development is critical. Did we not know of it by hearsay, the subject matter might never have been anticipated.

The dial needle, though, starts moving in this general direction from the earliest time. There had

always been a great curiosity and interest about
Europe, every part of it, even when Willa Cather
had been merely an unusually active child, growing
up freely on the Divide. Passage after passage in the
Nebraska novels, taken autobiographically, makes this
clear. Her first journey to the Old World, nevertheless, had come only in her twenty-ninth year, when
she went abroad from Pittsburgh with her friend
Isabelle McClung, in the summer of 1902.

In his *Willa Cather, a Critical Biography*, E. K.
Brown has summarized its Provençal days most sym-
pathetically (pages 103–4):

> In September they journeyed to the south,
> into the warm land of Alphonse Daudet, where
> the mistral blew "more terrible than any wind
> that ever came up from Kansas." Willa Cather
> drank in the warmth and color of the land and
> rejoiced in its people. The impressions of Pro-
> vence garnered now were ineffaceable to the last.
> She rejoiced in the landscape, the history, the
> architecture, the food, the wine; she stayed at
> the hotel in the ancient Papal city of Avignon,
> which Henry James had affectionately praised
> in his travel writings. Willa Cather and Isabelle
> McClung were the only English-speaking people
> in the town; there seemed to be no other tourists
> and Willa Cather enjoyed saturating herself with
> the life and aspect of the place. Here on the bank
> of the Rhône the young woman from the Divide
> had found something that touched her more
> deeply than the metropolitan density of London
> or the luminous quality of Paris; a life rooted
> in the centuries—what she later had in mind
> when she spoke of the things that lie deep behind
> French history and French art. That art extended
> to the sense of well-being that comes from sun

and light and artfully cooked food; it is reflected in Bishop Latour's remark when he tastes the soup cooked by Father Vaillant: ". . . a soup like this is not the work of one man. It is the result of a constantly refined tradition. There are nearly a thousand years of history in this soup."

Later he tells us (page 269): "The story she was writing in the last years of her life was to express what Avignon, the Avignon of the popes, had meant to her over a period of forty years." Its roots therefore grew deep; and rich living was to nourish them.

A decade later—but Willa Cather developed late, and slowly—presumably after the publication in 1912 of her first full-length, Jamesian tale, *Alexander's Bridge*, and while *O Pioneers!*, her first novel of the soil, was still in manuscript, she even assured her friend Elizabeth Shepley Sergeant, as we are told in the latter's *Willa Cather, a Memoir* (page 97), that "Some time . . . there would be a story with sharp clear definite lines like the country in which I then was [the South of France]." So we have an expressed intention, even at the beginning of a long and fertile career, which first would take her to very different regions. To use the classic expression of Sarah Orne Jewett, some story about Avignon had begun to tease her a full generation before she took it up in sober earnest.

To understand the powerful symbol for her work which Avignon became, with its overtone of religion and, above all, its particular expression of what to Willa Cather was true beauty, one must slowly follow the thread of her whole career. Patiently wound up, this will lead us through the labyrinth.

At the very beginning there is a major vacillation, which it took her a long while to work through. This came in the difficult Pittsburgh years (1896–1906), which Edith Lewis has judged, and no doubt rightly, to have been for a number of reasons among the hardest in her life. Too little considered has been her first book of short stories—in their original version—*The Troll Garden*, of 1905, which came exactly at the end of this period, and was its summation. A symmetrical pattern of alternation is so clear that, of the seven stories composing it, the first three odd-numbered are distinctly Jamesian, both in setting and delineation of character, while the three even ones were drawn with considerable courage and skill from her own bare world of the West. The seventh and concluding one, "Paul's Case," forms a separate and hybrid Pittsburgh epilogue. One could not ask for a better graphic representation of her differing experiments in the attempt to find her proper field.

The contents of the Jamesian first, third, and fifth stories of this book—"Flavia and Her Artists," "The Garden Lodge," and "The Marriage of Phaedra"—show that while she still was teaching high school in Pittsburgh, writing from Judge McClung's house where she was a guest, she must have imagined it almost obligatory for herself to attempt tales of worldly people of high fashion whom she could not possibly have known at this time, people of established place and assured means, preoccupied almost wholly in a dissection of their own emotions. These were the chic puppets of the hour; but were everywhere taken quite seriously.

In the first story, she writes of a large house party in Tarrytown, high life in an elaborate setting, maids and valets, a conservatory, a smoking-room with Turkish hangings and "curious weapons on the wall." The action of the second tale unrolls in "a place on the Sound," with "a glorious garden." It belongs to a man who when he married the heroine "had been for ten years a power in Wall Street." There a new summer house seems planned chiefly for another house party. In "The Marriage of Phaedra," set in London, we find people of title who come and go, casual mentions of Paris and Nice. Willa Cather seems determined to qualify as a sophisticate, although she has as yet come no farther from Red Cloud than Pittsburgh. Still, this was the fashion of the time; and as she devised them, these settings seemed proper even for popular consumption. "Society" in America was still enthroned by popular consent, nourished by general interest. We are in the period before it gave way to the romances of film stars; and its sins were told in every Sunday supplement.

Parenthetically, what is even more of a pure pastiche of Henry James exists. This is a story titled "Eleanor's House," published in *McClure's* for 1907 (Vol. XXIX), soon after Willa Cather had joined that magazine in New York. Here her protagonists have such complete leisure and are depicted as so removed from the hard facts of life in "their own place on the Oise" that, although one man is actually mentioned as "at work in the library," it is almost impossible to imagine what occupies him there. Such expatriate wraiths may want to "finish the summer in Switzerland" or even, as a final touch, be "very keen about going to America"—this from Willa Cather!— yet their behavior is altogether shadowy. Every description of the feel of a place, a stream, or a rampart brings her back to us; almost nothing else in this short story does.

In sharpest planned alternation with the tales, in *The Troll Garden,* of a life that even in the future never was to become her own, is the stark, tragic trilogy of the stories with a Western background. "A Wagner Matinée," "The Sculptor's Funeral," and "A Death in the Desert" all three represent already the

Willa Cather of the Nebraska Divide and the South-west whom we familiarly know, looking the grim fates boldly in the eye, competently grasping with both hands the tragedies of human destiny. "Paul's Case," the last in the book, in which she is so sensitively aware of dim hungers, takes her hero from a Pittsburgh variant of this drab world into that other, into the muffled luxury of the hotels, the perfume of hothouse flowers, the music, of snow-covered, wintry New York. Yet Paul must pay for this so brief pleasure by taking his own life. The alternation of a pair of powerfully beaten and contrasting rhythms with a final coda is perfect.

Quite curiously, at her next stage of development the whole search for a proper field has to be gone through once again—this time in full scale. There is exactly the same contrast, both in setting and sub-ject matter, between the worldly *Alexander's Bridge*, of 1912, and the rustic *O Pioneers!*, of the following year. How Willa Cather judged that these together also made a single unit, and how she had labored in giving them birth, she makes clear in a pregnant little essay of self-revelation contributed as late as 1931 to *Colophon, Part 6*. It was titled "My First Novels (There Were Two)."

Setting, however, as well as scale and depth, has now expanded. *Alexander's Bridge* gives us clear and capable pictures of the Back Bay in Boston, which, through her friendship with Mrs. James T. Fields, of unsurpassable literary memories, she now knew at first hand. Indeed, in it we almost enter Mrs. Fields's house, at the beginning of the book. There are also London scenes, no longer divined through others' eyes, but become much less mysterious to her through her work and travel there for *McClure's*. *O Pioneers!*, which is really a story of a Scandinavian farmer's daughter's love for Willa Cather's own wild land, definitely wins the upper hand, of course. Thus her career is finally launched, to rise to glorious heights. Willa Cather was now forty years old; at last free to fulfill her destiny and consume herself in her work, as once she had dreamed.

This is not the place to explore in detail the development of her internal feeling for the Nebraskan or the Virginian scene, the two that by inheritance she could fairly call her own. Here also there was much fluctuation: young fear and repulsion only very gradually transformed by a prolonged metamorphosis into their opposites. Against the materialism of the aftercomers alone, the second generation, that lesser breed after the pioneers, was she to remain adamant in lifelong hostility. Here were enemies she moved to slay whenever she rediscovered them. So we can at this place, without losing the clue, pass beyond *The Song of the Lark*, of 1915, and *My Ántonia*, published three years later.

There followed *Youth and the Bright Medusa*, in 1920, a book of collected short stories, in which she turned for new material to four pieces (three already published in magazines) about artists and their struggles—thus often speaking for herself—while at the same time reissuing the three earlier Western stories, somewhat revised, and also adding "Paul's Case," from *The Troll Garden*. This last book had long been out of print, and was now fifteen years behind her. "The Diamond Mine," "A Gold Slipper," and "Scandal" all concern the stage and have American settings; "Coming Aphrodite," new—and thus used to begin the book—represents her first days in Greenwich Village. We have in all of them the American scene of their decade, with steamships and motor cars to match; and there are only as many fleeting references to Europe as needed.

The contemporary world is now hers in this neat packet, with all the variants that she felt had permanent interest for her. Jamesian or Whartonian subjects, it is to be noted, in which she had earlier tried to qualify, are now sternly omitted; and one field she never entered: the chronicling of society for itself. Indeed, the only part of the Metropolitan Opera House she will apparently never touch, in spite of her long preoccupation with singers and their lives, is its Diamond Horseshoe.

From this satisfactory time, recapitulation achieved, a further—and for our present purposes most interesting—development begins. She embarks on a war story, *One of Ours*, which will take both us and herself from the later Nebraska, where the best seems already departed, over to France. On this novel of transition she worked for no less than four years. As for her hero, so for herself it was "The Voyage of the Anchises" (the title of one of its books), which bore her away from a familiar land to another where the adventure of life was to begin afresh, more glorious and with other vicissitudes. *One of Ours* was also published in what we shall see became a critical year of her life, 1922.

The story of the novel progresses from the shallowness of a mechanized Nebraska, deeply ugly and frustrating to a sensitive and inarticulate boy, pathetic in his stubborn loyalty to ideals that he cannot even define, across the seas to France, where he finds the fullness of his life in wonder, only a little before the war ends it. Here Willa Cather shows rare skill. The evocation of the church of Saint Ouen, in Rouen, for example, the crimson and purple colors of its rose window, its grave and deep-toned bell—we are simply taken there; we see and hear as through the just-awakened senses of diffident—oh, so diffident—youth. And the nearest approach to a true love affair in the book, Claude's meeting with Mademoiselle de Courcy —who represents so well the fineness of a tradition that even in Europe was to pass—how effectively this comes after the horror and trap of a completely loveless marriage, to a frigid and unseeing neighbor, back in Nebraska! There is a sureness amounting to divination as to what mattered, in the mature European point of view, and what did not. I do not believe that this sensitive juxtaposition of the American West with France, so fleeting and fragile, so quietly evocative of the highest loyalties of each, has yet been noticed for what it is.

The novel ends far away from where it began: with a grave in France for Claude, who "died believing his own country better than it is, and France better than any country can ever be." Here Willa Cather is also surely speaking for herself.

A few sentences later, at the book's close, she is impelled to the heights. "Perhaps it was as well to see that vision, and then to see no more." Suddenly the mood becomes absolutely black: "One by one the heroes of that war, the men of dazzling soldiership, leave prematurely the world they have come back to. Airmen whose deeds were tales of wonder, officers whose names made the blood of youth beat faster, survivors of incredible dangers,—one by one they quietly die by their own hand. Some do it in obscure lodging houses, some in their office, where they seem to be carrying on their business like other men. Some slip over a vessel's side and disappear into the sea." . . . "And they found," she concludes, "they had hoped and believed too much." The end of the war only clamped tighter upon American life the shackles of materialism which were for her a profanation and a torment. Her world had been so very near to a splendid liberation; and now it could lapse, slip back, into this!

Such feelings, I believe, help to explain a cryptic and critical sentence, as self-revelatory as any she ever wrote—Willa Cather was not given to enlargement of her personal feelings—that we find, fourteen years later (1936), in the Prefatory Note to *Not Under Forty*, a book of essays published in that year.

Here it is with its preceding context:

> The title of this book is meant to be "arresting" only in the literal sense, like the signs put up for motorists: "ROAD UNDER REPAIR" etc. It means that the book will have little interest for people under forty years of age. The world broke in two in 1922 or thereabouts, and the persons and prejudices recalled in these sketches slid back into yesterday's seven thousand years. . . ."

The painful disillusion, after what she had hoped would come from the war, had taken the usual eternity (to borrow the phrase she got from Stephen Crane) "to filter through the blood." Now, fourteen years later, she could submerge her personal disappointment within larger issues; she could take her stand, refusing to be budged from tested excellencies, refusing to yield to what she considered ignoble and inferior. She had been of her place and of her time, she would remain so; and if this meant lack of comprehension by the younger generation—in part, perhaps, matching hers also of them—well, they were warned, and could keep away. There is ferocity and bitterness here; but rather than march in the festal train of the Bitch Goddess of worldly success, she will pay any price, even that of alternating between public scorn and private silence. The world has caged her; but beware of her paws! There is to be no silliness about the matter.

Yet she was not permanently caged. A restless, splendid character such as hers would be bound, in the end, to escape—and did. From now on she begins ranging farther and farther afield. "Away, away, in time and space" seems to be her mood. After another book published in 1923, a penultimate glance at the Nebraska of her youth, four great novels succeed one another within the space of a single decade. The book of that year is familiar to many: *A Lost Lady*, a story of decline and fall, of elegiac reminiscence and of tender regret for vanished frailty. The "Lady" is also lost, one must observe, in the snows of yesteryear.

Then we come to the wayfarer's high plateau, where it is already afternoon with lengthening shadows, and a constant preoccupation over the meaning of life—and also with death at the end much nearer. The titles themselves are highly evocative. Here is the succession:

The Professor's House	(1925)
My Mortal Enemy	(1926)
Death Comes for the Archbishop	(1927)
Shadows on the Rock	(1931)

Note the allegory and symbolism in their wording. The Professor's true house, as his story makes abundantly clear, is his own grave; this is *his* long home. The enmity of Myra Henshawe for her husband, in the next novel, is maintained, indeed grows and battens, under miserably straitened and constricting circumstances that finally allow her only the manner of choosing her death. Then great Death itself—like a Holbein series, the grim procession continues—comes for the Archbishop in his cell near the desert; while in another austere region, rock-bound Quebec, we can watch shadows fall on further lives. There is no escape from pessimism, or at least from the firmest grasp on the realities of time and human destiny. As in the legend, in this last book, of the Canadian heiress who longed to become a recluse and then—ardors over—lapsed into terrible and prolonged aridity, every device that can be used presses the one inescapable conclusion: we are mortal, we must die.

The Professor's House, of 1925, as E. K. Brown has pointed out, is an allegory contrived with extraordinary skill, especially the mechanism of inserting a long *nouvelle* into the center of it, to give an effect of distant clarity and lyric beauty, of sunlit aerial color, seen beyond a dull, conventional foreground. Dead Tom Outland looms, sweet in the purity of young strength, towering beyond the pettiness of the life of a small academic community, where vulgar Louie Marsellus and his shallow wife revel in his succession. The Professor himself passes in the course of the story from later middle age, success achieved but becoming meaningless, into the much colder and passive region of his last years; and Willa Cather has fashioned him of exactly the same age as herself.

Nowhere is she cleverer than in the symbolism of the various houses that are so important to this story. There is the Professor's old house, where we see him first, the one he is so reluctant to leave, from the very beginning casting a lingering look behind—jerry-built and uncomfortable, but a place where there had been deep and joyful living. There is the new house that can never have true life infused into it; he has even lost his love for the woman who will be its mistress. We are given glimpses also of the elaborate monstrosity of the Marsellus ménage, tricked out with money inherited from the dead Tom Outland, and even named —a profanation—with his last name, used as a wretched pun. Tom's own group of cliff dwellers' houses, the houses that he has discovered, simple and intrinsically beautiful, thus makes the clearest contrast between spurious values and those high and ancient ones that can outlast calamity. Finally the Professor's house-to-be, his grave, completes the grim symbolism.

Willa Cather can be very direct in such matters. After a close call from accidental death through sheer and symptomatic lethargy, she makes the Professor reflect that his sagging old couch is already his coffin, with poor sham upholstery: "Just the equivocal American way of dealing with serious facts," she says. "Why pretend that it is possible to soften that last hard bed?" No palliative, no trickery or ornamentation will blind her to the essential hardness, to the punishments of life. She will have none of the cheap standards, the petty consolations, about her.

In terminating his own discussion of the book (on page 246), E. K. Brown makes a significant remark: "Not by any answers it proposes, but by the problems it elaborates, and by the atmosphere in which they are enveloped, *The Professor's House* is a religious novel." So we have come out onto the last great plateau of Willa Cather's own journey. She is now much nearer to a finish with the local scene and its rather minuscule passions, which she has definitely appraised.

The development continues inevitably, inexorably. One of the hardest, most obstinate stories of her whole work is the relatively short, but strangely intense, novel published in 1926 (only one year later, and in her own fifty-third), *My Mortal Enemy*. It remains a mysterious work. E. K. Brown, who must long have pondered its cryptic subject matter, does suggest a clue. In the end, he says (page 250): ". . . it becomes plain to us that this worldly woman has passed out of worldliness into preoccupation with primary realities."⁷ This is the place to which Willa Cather wanted to bring her heroine, after headstrong youth and an ill-considered elopement with a much weaker man, whose character could never match her own. Finally Myra goes straight to religion, which here is not treated by implication, as in *The Professor's House*, or even as an anodyne, consoling the end to the unhappy life of a once worldly woman, of fierce will power, *détraquée*. Here it becomes a principal part of the story. The way now opens for the next two, perhaps the greatest pair of Willa Cather's novels.

A light ever seems to radiate from broad sun-swept stretches in the Southwestern desert landscape of *Death Comes for the Archbishop* (1927). There is also a marvelous unity to the book, made up in large part of deceptively simple passages; here a local story re-told, there a pious legend remembered. To this corresponds the harmonious and expanded character of Father Latour himself. In part he may be taken to represent Willa Cather's own late summer hours—or at least her aspiration for them—in the country she had discovered far beyond her old West, in one of the great adventures of her intellectual life.

What is significant in the new direction of her journey—which through much reminiscence of Auvergne, the province from which both priests in the book had started, becomes also a pilgrimage in the direction of Avignon—is that she now is a declared seeker for a faith that will console her, nostalgic as she always has been, for the perishability of life. Indeed, that life of "The Best Years"—the title of a very touching later tale—had passed first, as Virgil had phrased it in words that she long held in memory.

For her, also, *"Optima dies . . . prima fugit. . . ."*
It is significant also that in the year 1922, when
the geological break in the continuity of her life had
occurred, in that year she herself entered the Episcopal
church, being confirmed at the same time as her parents. As is Episcopal to Baptist, it would seem, so is
the great beauty of what once was and now is gone to
the more prosaic world of the present. Yet her treat-
ment of Catholics in this book, as well as later in
Shadows on the Rock, became so sympathetic as she
went along that many readers quite unconsciously must
have thought her speaking for her own faith—which
in a sense she was. She has indeed already moved her
setting far away from her own youth and early novels.

Death Comes for the Archbishop also constantly
takes one backward and forward, on missions of religion, between the Old World and the New; it is as if
Willa Cather were intent upon weaving a cable of
many strands between them. She seems to delight in
flashing before us the scenery of Rome or Clermont,
intermittently, to contrast them with Sante Fé or Taos;
demonstrating that the greatest discrepancies vanish,
and only harmonies remain, for those who are dedicated
to a great ideal and thus in part transcend their surroundings. Here, on such firm heights, the unhappy
and restive self perishes, to give way at the last to
harmony and tranquillity. Vicariously this was her
coming to terms with her own destiny. It further ex-
plains her intention behind the disarming and lovable
simplicity of the small events in the foreground of the
novel, symbols that with the economy of a great artist
she has used for great purposes.

Colder, later in personal time, and more remote also
by more than a century—for the action is set in the
time of Louis XIV—is the next story, the serious, not

to say somber, *Shadows on the Rock,* of 1931. Willa Cather is now in her fifty-eighth year. Her heroine is a young, motherless girl whose somewhat frail life revolves almost wholly about her touching effort to achieve a woman's warmth and service for the household of an aging father. The characters of Count Frontenac and Monseigneur Laval are drawn as those of already old men.

The bastion of the great rock on which Quebec has been founded, the climate, the cold winters, somehow all seem of an unvarying gray after the smiling warmth of the open Southwest. Here and there a sheen as of unexpected late sunset wonderfully suffuses her mood; although Willa Cather herself seems to have moved still farther away, both in time and space. Religion also is very near the heart of this book. The characters are American in the sense that they come to live permanently in the New World—although even Cécile, her young heroine, is represented as born in Paris—but their pathos is in their continuing attempt, destined for never more than partial success, to transplant and keep alive, under hard and adverse conditions, the standards of the full civilization of France, their distant and revered *"mère des arts et des lettres."* This must be accomplished in a world where even the flora and fauna are as on another planet, often menacing as in a nightmare.

Willa Cather makes much of Old World cooking, of cleaning and polishing, of the amenity of a sensitive and quiet bourgeois *"foyer."* By the night fireside in the little house on the crooked street the old values still have force and power. The latent threat comes from the genius of the new land itself; and the ships that sail slowly across the stormy seas, and whose arrival becomes as vital to the reader as it is for the inhabitants of Quebec itself, these ships bear the very life-blood that must continually be transfused if what was admirable and remembered can continue under such difficulties.

Subtly Willa Cather's sympathies seem to have changed; or is it such a change, after all, because from the earliest time her German musicians, her young men from Prague—or Bergen or Upsala—even arriving as poor immigrants, these had brought to the outlying farms about Red Cloud values that the young girl who was also Willa Cather sensed by every worthy measurement as far transcending what they found in possession about them. Excellence does not change, whatever the circumstances, the fluctuations in its appreciation.

As so often after a major advance Willa Cather now seems to need rest on her flinty journey. There comes about a time of retrospect; first with the three stories collected in the volume titled *Obscure Destinies* (1932), and in the sensitive portrayal of touching *Lucy Gayheart* (1935), a last full-length evocation of the world of her morning years. Then, going back even earlier, she turns to the dim days of her earliest childhood in Virginia, this last a theme scarcely touched before—indeed, except as a background it had not determined her life. As is to be expected, the development proceeds step by step with a decline in her own vitality.

She had early rebelled against her destiny, born on the fringe of things; she had defied, she had never surrendered. Now she seems to wish passionately to submit. The violins tune to some of the most beautiful melodies of all: in "Old Mrs. Harris," a tale in *Obscure Destinies*, she can touch sublimity—can create it out of almost nothing. The same is just as true of another touching and so delicate short story, already mentioned, "The Best Years," published posthumously

in *The Old Beauty*. It is also about the earliest Western
time, but now seen as far behind and long ago vanished. The journey may be wilder, the hour late, and
there is no "going home" now except to death; yet
courage and love have not failed her.

The place of *Sapphira and the Slave Girl*, begun in
1937 and published only in 1941, four years later and
in her own sixty-seventh, is curious. It is a cold, slow-
paced book, the chief character a willful and repellent
invalid. One receives the impression that the material
was never turned to in affection—at least, with the
old spontaneous and warm affection that Willa Cather
could give to the destiny of Ántonia, who had been
such a match for her fate—but rather in an attempt,
a decision, to cultivate one more area that she knew
well but never had used. The action occurs near Win-
chester, Virginia, and the uneventful year is 1856.

This novel, as E. K. Brown comments (page 317),
is not about "heroic moments in American life—the
moment when the French made a civilization in the
Canadian wilderness, the moment when the Southwest was at its apex, the moment when the wild land
of Nebraska took the first impress of the pioneer.
Now it was enough to evoke quite ordinary moments
from the past; and these too had vanished, taking with
them the burden of beauty for which there was nothing to compensate."

It almost seems as if Willa Cather had come to a
dead end; and indeed this may have been so, for in
illness and fatigue she published nothing else during
the seven years remaining before her death in April
1947, in her seventy-fourth year.

At this point the story about Avignon consequently
takes on added interest. For Willa Cather apparently
attempted her most difficult task, the summoning of

reality from a remotely distant time and place, which in any event she never could have known personally —as in some measure she did know something about all that had gone before—when life had most worn and tired her. So the circumstances surrounding the work were somber and not very favorable. Personally, she was facing the adamant combination of old age, illness, and the slow approach of death—that ultimate engagement in which triumph was impossible. Perhaps also she reached the field of the tale in a historical setting just too late: energies never sufficed, we must remember, over seven years, to bring it to completion. And this may have been one of the reasons— which we must respect—why at the end she ordered its destruction.

Even if she surmised that her powers were failing, she may still have wanted the companionship and solace of a piece of work in the making, as it always had been for her in the richer years of her own life. To work, also, was to pray. This may explain what was going on in her mind when we see her as Edith Lewis describes her, pacing the "open roof garden of the Fairmont, walking to and fro, and reading. . . ." Okey's little guide-book becomes a breviary.

It is easy to see why a French palace like that at Avignon rather than the one at Versailles should have seized on Willa Cather's imagination. Her firmly expressed distastes would normally find the latter artificial and flimsy, just where the noble pile beside the Rhône was the reverse. The surprise and splendor of the conception, the wonderful spareness of the lofty architecture, these broad halls set high above rich farming-land, this capital of popes in exile, across the mountains and beside a broad, rushing Provençal river: all would have spoken clarion words.

Constant similarities between the rural life of Provence and regions she had known all her life in the

West must also have been in mind. Farming is farming: to plow and to sow, to harvest and to garner, require the same labor, take their toll with the same fatigue, no matter by whom performed, where—or when. Yet there were also the particular vigor and sap of this people. From her own twenty-ninth year, now long in the past, she had been consciously drawn to their special character, which apparently never ceased to delight her.

Once the definite conception had taken shape, she did, for a while, proceed. As Edith Lewis tells us (pages 195–6):

> She worked fitfully at the Avignon story in the next two years [i.e., 1944 and 1945]; but her right hand was so troublesome [with a long disability that set in], became instantly so painful when she tried to write, that she was unable to make much headway. It was a story of large design, and needed concentrated vigour and power. Her knowledge of this often led her to put it aside entirely and try to forget about it until better times should come.

Alas, they did not; and now even this incomplete manuscript is destroyed.

Why, we must ask, did she at the last thus turn so completely away from America? The fact that the world had broken apart for her personally in 1922 has become clear enough. That in *One of Ours* she turned savagely against the American present is attested by the dark flow at the end of the book. She also reverts to this same theme in the story about "The Old Beauty," which, although written earlier, was only published posthumously, in 1948. Here she sets her story wholly in Aix-les-Bains—how unthinkable this would have been earlier in her career!—which her middle-aged American finds, to his satisfaction, "unchanged" in a world already transformed; and this story is also set in the fateful year of 1922.

She is no longer at any pains to conceal her disillusion and aversion to most of the life about her. For a writer as classic both in feeling and style as Willa Cather, this judgment was natural enough. Indeed, in her private life she took no trouble to conform to newer interests about her, in literature, or art, or music. To preserve her entity, in a time of too facile communication, she became almost a recluse, certainly not "keeping up" with contemporary movements. Her defense was dogged and complete. She does, in the essay titled "A Chance Meeting," in *Not Under Forty*, qualify Marcel Proust as "the greatest French writer of his time"; but otherwise one hears of no later enthusiasms whatsoever. She will not go beyond Thomas Mann and Katherine Mansfield. Indeed, in the last months of her life she turned away from everything of the present, back even to Shakespeare and to Chaucer. Here was her grandeur and her consolation.

A soliloquy in the critical *One of Ours* should at this point be recalled. Of her hero, Claude, she says (page 406):

He had begun to believe that the Americans were a people of shallow emotions. That was the way [his friend] Gerhardt had put it once; and if it was true, there was no cure for it. Life was so short that it meant nothing at all unless it were continually reinforced by something that endured; unless the shadows of individual existence came and went against a background that held together.

Thus France could give one meaning to life which it was impossible to find in America.

It could not have been easy, nevertheless, for her to turn to Europe, to expatriate herself—even if only spiritually—as had Henry James and Edith Wharton (although for very different reasons) before her. Even for them, as we know, the task was of immense magnitude and yielded dubious results; and they were wealthy patricians who without great effort could remove themselves from any place to any other. Willa Cather, embedded as she had been in Nebraska, and with a much harder destiny in many ways than those of such comparative darlings of fortune, took much longer; but in the end and by gradual steps she did very nearly the same thing. Like many people of plain origins, her first great need had been to be reassured, to still the youthful panic of seeming to possess only an inferior brand of everything that her more fortunate brothers and sisters took as naturally theirs. This was a prime need; but she had conquered it in her own way, which was the way of genius.

Furthermore, Edith Wharton and Henry James lived much the same cosmopolitan life wherever they happened to be, following—even when they were railing at—contemporary fashion. Willa Cather reached first for the stars over the pure air of Nebraska, and then, when their light became obscured, would accept nothing less beautiful in their place simply because it was American. Her position was grander; the evolution of vastly more moment. Her stubborn loyalty to excellence, and the tenderness of her love, refused to alter because they had come upon alteration. Thus the Avignon story, incomplete and vanished as it is, remains the last great testimony of what she believed in, and of what she had lived for.

We should have to conclude on this lofty but rather barren note were is not for a piece of singular good fortune, a circumstance that is the origin of this essay.

Miss Lewis does remember quite a little of the manuscript that no longer exists; and she has been kind
enough to give the following account of it, thus adding
a precious last chapter to the history of Willa Cather's
writing:

> The title of Willa Cather's unfinished and un-
> published Avignon story was *Hard Punishments*.
>
> The setting was Avignon of the 14th century
> (1340), at the time of the papal residence of Bene-
> dict XII.
>
> The central characters were two youths—whom
> she tentatively called Pierre and André; and the
> story was of their friendship.
>
> It opened with a scene on the height above the
> Papal Palace, overlooking the Rhône. This place
> is now a park; but in the 14th century it was a
> sort of ash-heap, where refuse from the Palace was
> thrown over the cliff. Pierre, a peasant boy from
> a farm beyond the river, has climbed up there in
> order to sit and look across toward his former
> home. He is a criminal, according to the law of
> the time. A simple, childlike, rather stupid boy—
> he had traded off his father's cart and donkey,
> and a load of pottery he was carrying to market,
> for a wonderful monkey belonging to a sailor
> who was passing through the town. His father had
> denounced him for theft to the authorities, and as
> punishment he was strung up for several hours
> by his thumbs. His hands are now useless, and he
> is an outcast—homeless, in constant pain, and
> unable to work. A woman in the town who keeps
> a brothel has taken him in and given him a corner
> in which to sleep. He sits on the height above the
> Palace, crying from homesickness and misery.
>
> It is the day on which Benedict XII, on his
> great stallion, surrounded by a magnificent train,

has gone down to meet Alfonso of Castile and his embassy, who have ridden from Spain to seek an indulgence from the Pope. The Palace is half empty, for many of its occupants, and most of the townspeople of Avignon, have flocked to see the splendid meeting.

While the peasant boy sits crying on his ash-heap, he hears a noise of breaking branches in the hedge that divides this spot from the Papal gardens; and there emerges the other youth in the story—André.

This boy is handsome, spirited, intelligent, well-born—his uncle holds an important post among the servitors in the Palace. But he cannot speak. His tongue has been torn out as a punishment for blasphemy.

Willa Cather was greatly interested in the subject of blasphemy, as it was regarded in the 14th century. It was not only a sin, but a crime, and was punished by the civil law. According to the records, it was a rather frequent transgression, in spite of the terrible punishment for it. Why was it held in such special reprobation? And why, in spite of the risk, did people so often succumb to the temptation to blaspheme?

Some time before the meeting of the two boys, there had been a great banquet in the Papal Palace. André had certain special duties to perform; but when they were over, he slipped away and joined a group of wild companions in the town, with whom he had lately become involved—in a sense a revolutionary group, who met in a low dive to air subversive theories against the Church and State. Excited by the daring of their reckless talk, André tries to out-do the others. The dive was that night spied on by the police, and André and his companions were reported and punished.

Tearing out the tongue with red-hot pincers was the usual punishment for blasphemy.

A scene is given in which an old blind priest, who had been André's friend and confessor since the boy's childhood, comes to him after his ordeal, where he lies tossing on his cot in his cubicle in the Palace, talks to the frantic boy, comforts him, fortifies him, and absolves him. This was perhaps the central scene in the story.

My own understanding of it (I never discussed it with Miss Cather) was that she meant the deep root of the boy's despair to be, not the disgrace, nor even the mutilation, but his sense of a sort of personal dishonor—of having irretrievably betrayed something sacred in himself, thereby making the future impossible. The priest's compassionate reassurance enables him to take up his life again. And when he does so, it is on a new plane. His disability becomes for him a challenge —to his courage and resourcefulness, to his pride. After his encounter with Pierre, the poor peasant boy becomes a part of this challenge. He sets out to succor, perhaps to rescue, one even more unfortunate than himself.

The latter part of the story was told only in notes, and was not completed.

It is with hesitation that I have given even this brief account—for it is like the story of an opera without the music. How much would a short summary of *My Ántonia* or *Old Mrs. Harris* mean to one who could never by any possibility read them? Whatever elements of beauty and power the unfinished Avignon story may have possessed —they are lost to us now. But to the student of Willa Cather's work these notes may be of interest in indicating the tenor of her thoughts and the direction her genius took in the last years.

With the help of this precious information we at least now possess an outline of the unfinished story. There is a further treasure that Miss Lewis with great kindness has also made available to the author, Willa Cather's own much-marked copy of "Okey's little history": *The Story of Avignon*, by Thomas Okey [Mediaeval Towns Series], London, J. M. Dent and Sons, Ltd., 1926.

Here we come wonderfully close to the creative process; for not only is this book much marked with single and even double lines in the margins, and further with checks and crosses; but on the last flyleaf and the inside of the back cover, in Willa Cather's own hand we have half a dozen—seven, to be exact—notations of what became of special importance for her in planning this tale. A study of these brings illumination. We come very close to the times in which she placed her story, to its setting, and no little detail of its circumstances.

First of all, there is the problem of the years in which it occurred. Inside the back cover she has noted "Benedict XII" by name, and also written out the years of his reign: "1334 to 1342." She has also placed opposite this two references to the text, one to page 93, where one of his biographers describes him—he had been born Jacques Fournier, in the County of Foix, and first became a Cistercian monk—as "hard, obstinate, avaricious; he loved the good overmuch and hated the bad; he was remiss in granting favours, and negligent in providing for the services of the Church; more addicted to unseemly jests than to honest conversation; he was a mighty toper and '*Bibamus papaliter*—let us drink like a pope'—became a proverb in his day."

On page 88, which she has further noted and even circled, we find this description: "Pope Benedict . . . was a big man and *molto corpulento*. He was a most

holy man who never would give dispensation for
marriage between kinsfolk, and was careful and dili-
gent in searching the moral characters of all candidates
for benefices, and many he examined himself. *Non
bolea ideote*—he would have no illiterates—he went
about seeking good and efficient clerics, and honoured
them much because he found so few." How clear it
is that a man of this stamp would have drawn her
interest!

Benedict XII, though, is not the only pope mentioned inside the back cover. Willa Cather there has
also written down the year "1305"—merely the four
ciphers; but she gives a reference for this date to page
44 of the text, where she has marked a sentence reading: "On June 5, 1305, after eleven months of obscure
intrigue and patent discord, Raymond of Goth, Archbishop of Bordeaux, was elected to the papal chair, and
assumed the title of Clement V." We now know that
she definitely placed her story within the first half of
the fourteenth century and in the reign of Benedict
XII, but perhaps at one stage it was to have at least a
start in this earlier time.

"Law" and "Prisons" are words that she has also
noted in this place, both of them referring to the same
page, 242. Here a corner is turned down, and on this
and the pages following there are marks showing con-
centrated attention. On page 243 she notices and
marks, among a list of punishments inflicted in 1328
and 1329—only a few years previous to the accession
of Benedict XII—not one but two mentions of the
tearing out of tongues, the first with red-hot pincers,
the second for the crime of "swearing against the
Virgin Mary."

On the page following, 244, there are not less than
two lines and two checks marked opposite part of the
text giving the detail of crimes publicly denounced:
"Promulgated by a papal government, they naturally

begin with penalties against the denial of God, or of the Virgin Mary, or blaspheming against these or God's saints, or profane swearing at play or in taverns or the public streets. . . ." Willa Cather has documented herself securely on the "hard punishments" of the time.

Next we come to the setting; and for this there is a whole series of markings, too detailed to be transcribed—but showing how she had made herself familiar with the whole complex fabric of the papal palace and the various stages of its building. She notices on page 20, with a double line, "the great stone conduit which drained the kitchen into the Sorgue. . . ." On page 223 she has put a check opposite a mention recording payment "for carving four apes of stone in human form to be placed . . . over the portal of the palace," which we learn served as gargoyles. The creative process is feeling its way. Indeed, the whole of Okey's Chapter XV, part of which was titled "Life in a Mediaeval City," has been carefully worked over: it is much marked. One can see clearly how from a few suggestive sentences she brooded deep into her story.

The famous bridge across the Rhône apparently fascinated her. She first notices, with a checking on page 25, the community of Friars Hospitallers, founded "to establish ferriers, build bridges, and give hospitality to travellers along the rivers of Provence." She checks heavily on this same page a sentence reading: "Now, since the Pont St. Benezet was the only stone bridge between Lyons and the sea, until the building of the Pont St. Esprit in 1309, the importance it conferred on Avignon may easily be conceived."

The whole medieval town had become familiar. On page 305 she has especially marked the following description:

. . . a scene of incomparable beauty awaits us at the end of the shady walk that rises from the platform to the modern Promenade du Rocher des Doms. This, once the barren, wind-swept acropolis of Avignon which was crowned in papal times with the windmills and the forts, . . . and which in floodtime served as a cemetery, has been transformed into a delightful garden. . . . The view from the Belvedere over the Rhone and four departments of France is remarkable both for range and beauty. At our feet sweeps the broad majestic Rhone, hastening seaward *per aver pace co' seguaci sui,* and embracing in its course the great island of la Barthelasse with the remaining arches of the bridge, and the chapel of St. Nicholas; opposite are the hills and mountains of Languedoc, their nearer slopes, above poor dilapidated Villeneuve, fallen from her ancient splendour. . . . far in the background stands the square tower of Chateauneuf des Papes.

So this was the setting, familiar to her over many years, in which Willa Cather planned the encounter of her two boys: here there were space and breadth, distances of her own kind.

How she would have set about to make the region vivid, with all the charm of its trees and flowers— details in which she always took so much interest—is also certain. Earlier in the book, on page 5, a double line scores these sentences:

At Valence the dark cypress and her spire—that sentinel of the south—comes into view; the mulberry, the olive, the almond, the chestnut, the oleander, the myrtle, the ilex and the stone-pine, tell of sunnier skies. Even the common flowers of the north are transfigured under the magic of the bright, translucent sky. . . .

There is a very urgent marking on page 229—two lines with a check between—of the whole of the following paragraph:

> Among the amenities of the old palace were the spacious and lovely gardens on the east, with their clipped hedges, avenues of trees, flower-beds and covered and frescoed walls, all kept fresh and green by channels of water. John XXII maintained a menagerie of lions and other wild and strange beasts; stately peacocks swept proudly along the green swards, for the inventory of 1369 specifies seventeen peacocks, some old and some young, whereof six are white.

In one monastery garden, page 348, a "tall hedge of laurel 'high as a pine tree' " is further noted. The pencil mark is proof of her admiration.

That events could be made gorgeous in a setting such as this is in no doubt; and there was apparently also no little meditation on medieval feasting and carousal. Much marked and checked is a long passage, pages 237–8, abbreviated below:

> . . . The most striking example of lavish splendour is afforded by the State banquet given to Clement V by the Cardinals Arnaud de Palegrue and Pierre Taillefer in May 1308: Clement, as he descended from his litter, was received by his hosts and twenty chaplains, who conducted him to a chamber hung with richest tapestries from floor to ceiling; he trod on velvet carpet of triple pile; his state bed was draped with fine crimson velvet, lined with white ermine; the sheets of silk were embroidered with silver and gold. The table was served by four papal knights and twelve squires [this last word circled by Willa Cather

in the text—could it have been a possible role for André?], who each received silver girdles and purses filled with gold from the hosts: fifty cardinals' squires assisted them in serving the banquet, which consisted of nine courses of three plates each—twenty-seven dishes in all. The meats were built up in fantastic form: castles, gigantic stags, boars, horses, etc. . . . Then followed a concert of sweetest music, and dessert was furnished by two trees—one of silver, bearing rare fruits of all kinds, and the other loaded with sugared fruit of many colours. Various wines were then served, whereupon the master cooks, with thirty assistants, executed dances before the guests. . . .

A triumphal entry in 1340, a solemn embassy from Alphonso the Brave, King of Portugal, and his ally Alphonso of Castile, is also given special notice. This date is repeated in Miss Cather's hand on the margin of the passage, checked and scored, on page 89; and now we know that it was, effectively, the one determined upon for her story. "As the glittering pageant approached Avignon," we read in Okey, "red-robed cardinals went forth to meet it; a solemn pontifical mass was celebrated by Benedict himself, who preached a fine sermon. . . ."

Thus the material accumulated and took shape in her mind, to furnish a rich backdrop for the simple tale Willa Cather obviously wished—perhaps even in very strong contrast—to place against this splendor. On page 236 there are marked sentences mentioning ermine and beaver, payments to Tuscany for silk, for brocade to Venice: "The richness of the papal utensils beggars description: jewelled cups, flagons of gold, knife handles of jasper and ivory, forks of mother-of-pearl and gold. . . ." There was plenty to choose from. She marks a passage on page 221 mentioning "chests and cupboards for the silver vessels and scarlet of our lord the pope." A bell, also on this page, seems to have been of special interest, the "pontifical bell, which from its silvery tone was known as the *cloche d'argent.*" One recalls those in *One of Ours* and in *Death Comes for the Archbishop.* By her nature Willa Cather is conditioned to notice once more—here in medieval France—the objects that always had evoked most meaning.

She was not drawn, however, merely by descriptions of richness. On page 71 she has checked and underlined a mention of the no less than 65,000 letters relating to the reign of John XXII on the Vatican registers. The same underlining is found a little earlier, page 66, to notice the Pope's marshall, "one Walsingham, an Englishman." Thrice marked is this passage on page 239: ". . . amid all this luxury, strange defects of comfort appear to the modern sense. Windows, as we have seen [and Willa Cather has also put a mark opposite the previous mention earlier in the book, on page 218], were generally covered with waxed cloth or linen; carpets were rare, and rushes were strewn on the floors of most of the rooms."

A last item, which nonetheless heads the seven tabulated inside the back cover, must not go unmentioned. It is cryptic, reading only "Toulouse 170." If we turn to this page, which is also turned down at the corner, we find that it refers to the later reign of Pope Urban V (1362–70). The single sentence mentioning Toulouse states that this pope "loved learning, founded colleges and bursaries for poor students; he cared for the amenity of the services of the papal chapel, and sent a music master and seven boys to study music and singing at Toulouse."

Might it just possibly be that this was one way in which Willa Cather could have made the unfinished story develop, later sending her younger boy away to another city—even helped by the mute—thus to fulfill himself in song? We have far too little evidence to present this as more than a mere possibility; but the fact that the name of this other city, across France, heads the list of her seven mentions may be significant.

A strong caution is needed at this point. Miss Lewis has written to the author mentioning "how *little* of the historical material [above] Miss Cather actually introduced in the story . . . few of her stories have been so completely démeublé. There was almost no description; two or three paragraphs about the Palace itself—as she felt it rather than as it appeared; half a dozen words about Benedict XII, as he rode down to meet Alfonso. . . . The only room she described at all was the roasting kitchen in the Palace. No costumes, no functions. And yet, she managed to give the feeling of the place and time—I suppose because she herself felt it all so strongly."

So the technique of making the reader sense very much more than he is actually told—chiefly because it has been passed through the alembic of a powerful imagination, and there has been reduced to quintessence—this technique, one surmises, here was used by Willa Cather in the completest control of her great powers. To have taken everything possible in; but then calmly to cut most of it out: this is a procedure she had pressed to extremest use, as she herself has told us, even with the actual pounds of manuscript that she discarded from *Sapphira and the Slave Girl*. Here her subject was incomparably richer; and her scale was planned—as Miss Lewis recalls—to be merely that of a long *nouvelle*.

We have come a long distance indeed from the Willa Cather of her earlier years, from imitative experiment in the long ago—as in "Eleanor's House"—and from the first attempts to find herself; to find, above all, in Dostoevsky's phrase, who she was; and then to learn the secrets of her own art, her own creation.

At first one may see in this Avignon story many differences from the bulk of that earlier work. Certainly we are far from the wind-swept stretches of the Nebraska Divide, from nineteenth-century pioneers, the struggling farmers, the immigrant "hired girls." No one here is caught in the ugliness and problems of the present; we are under other skies and in quite another place. Yet if one dwells with the subject for even a little while, one becomes aware that in this Avignon story there must have been far less difference from Willa Cather's earlier work than might at first appear. The setting exists for an almost familiar group of circumstances. Far from entering a past where the ills of life have been mitigated and struggle washed away, pressures have only become more literal, the pains and penalties of living more direct. Religion, in this papal setting, seems also neither more nor less present than it has been for some time.

The title alone, *Hard Punishments*, affects a wonderful affiliation with past work. All of Willa Cather's characters know suffering, know handicap, know the hardness of life. It was the only fundamental circumstance, apparently, that interested her and seemed real to her; and this may be one of the reasons why she never—without exception—in her mature work, dealt with those born rich and privileged, who in so many ways therefore had nothing to struggle for; or at least whose private goals, in a totally different living habit, were to her unknown territory.

If one goes back in retrospect, even Alexander, the bridge-builder of the first novel, is observed and selected by her because of the fatal punishment that was to overtake him. In that early time her philosophy was already direct enough: "Some get a bad hurt early and lose their courage; and some never get a fair wind," says his old teacher, of the failures of life. It is all there thus at the beginning, even to the classical concision of her summary.

Ántonia's lot was hard. So was that of Thea; so was Lucy Gayheart's. Myra Henshawe's fate was adamant. In their destinies Claude and the Professor finally move into the region of death, where Tom Outland has gone before them. The ancient people of the Southwest, ages before, had only known the lesson perhaps better. In *The Song of the Lark*, the brewer's son discusses this with Thea: ". . . You mean the idea of standing up under things, don't you, meeting catastrophe? No fussiness." Willa Cather indeed knows what she herself means. In the Avignon story she in no way changed her course; indeed, she only reaffirmed it by giving to pain and suffering a simpler physical expression. Life without them would be impossible. "Old Mrs. Harris" states this definitively: "Everything that's alive has got to suffer." The law is as true in one time as in another.

So it seems as if, rather than shift from the only material she felt important, rather than move into the diminished lives of a younger—and, to her, petty—generation at home, Willa Cather remained true to her principles simply by abandoning America, the later America that she so castigated, as a setting. It was to bypass the morass of shallowness, to avoid a sense of decline, a pervading feeling of insignificance and triviality, that she moved her scene away; now we know with how little essential shift of interest. To capitalize on old success, to be static, or continue a familiar pattern, these were for her the fundamental impossibilities.

There is one change, however, that should be noted. Miss Lewis has thought that the action of the Avignon story might only have been meant to last for less than a year; and that its length was to be somewhat like that of *My Mortal Enemy*. In this setting of an expanded *nouvelle*, Willa Cather apparently wanted to deal with youth once more. We seem to have come through a tunnel, with the longer novels dealing with the end of life, with old age, its gloom and its decline. These, in retrospect, seem behind. It may be that here also, to quote a sentence in "Before Breakfast," the short story written after 1942 and published after her death in *The Old Beauty*, she feels that "Plucky youth is more bracing than enduring age." Certainly it is youth that Willa Cather is again considering; and almost certainly, in the end, youth triumphant. We thus come to our close on a fine, clear note, securely—though with transcendent compassion; even if the actual termination, as in Schubert's "Unfinished Symphony," was destined never to be written.

This incomplete story, then, does show a progression beyond the last point reached in Willa Cather's published work, beyond not only *Sapphira and the Slave Girl*, but also the two stories in the volume of *The Old Beauty* that stress the penalties of old age. As in the central story of that book, she has gone back to "The Best Years" once more. Enormous and mature power now long had been hers; there was indeed more to say, even in this setting, unthinkable at the beginning of her career. Life was being divined, strong situations created, even across the centuries. Essentially, however, the material has not changed. The problems were still those that had absorbed even her earliest characters; and these new ones set about to solve theirs in ways with which she now has made us familiar. Far from proving a refuge from the ills of the present, her new field reveals penalties only more intense than in the past, with greater challenge—but with response still adequate. From their own "hard punishments" her shadowy lads would undoubtedly have wrested the inner strength, one feels, that would have made them matches for their destiny. At the end, therefore, even in this unfinished story set in medieval Avignon, Willa Cather simply remains herself.

WILLA CATHER (1873-1947) was born near Win-
chester, Virginia. When she was ten, her family
moved from the peace of Virginia to the wild prairies
of Nebraska. She was graduated from the University of
Nebraska at twenty-one, and did newspaper work and
teaching in Pittsburgh, Pennsylvania, for the next few
years. She published a book of verse, April Twilights,
in 1903, and a book of short stories, The Troll Garden,
in 1905. They were followed, over the years, by twelve
novels, including Death Comes for the Archbishop and
Shadows on the Rock; four volumes of short stories,
and two volumes of essays.